# HAVEN RIVER

## BY CASEY FAE HEWSON

Cover design by Lynn O'Shea

Freshfields Graphic Design

Info@ffieldsdesign.co.nz


ISBN: 978-0-473-35560-9 (softcover)

ISBN: 978-0-473-35561-6 (Epub)

ISBN: 978-0-473-35562-3 (Kindle)

ISBN: 978-0-473-35563-0 (PDF)

ISBN: 978-0-473-35564-7 (ibook)

To VB

for encouraging me to keep going when it all
seemed too hard

# Part 1

Autumn is a second spring where every leaf is a flower.

Albert Camus

# Chapter 1

Luke paused, angling his head closer to the house, waiting for the inevitable.

And yep, there it was.

"Luke! Get your butt in here. Where's the lettuce? Hurry up."

"Yeah, yeah, yeah." Luke yanked a lettuce out of the veggie garden.

Time. His older brother Ryan's obsession with being on time or early drove Luke nuts. Luke did what he needed to do, and got where he needed to go – eventually. What did it matter if he was late? He hated having to do things on time, be somewhere at a certain hour. Why couldn't people just let him be?

Minky nuzzled Luke's hand and munched the lettuce.

"Oh, Minky." Luke rapped the goat lightly on her back. "That was for us, silly goat."

Minky chewed on, her eyelashes blinking in time to the lazy rustle of the trees. Luke wiped his forehead and pushed his cap further back on his head. He plucked another lettuce, and strolled past Marcus's latest car project and into the kitchen, reciting a half-finished poem under his breath.

Ten minutes later confusion reigned as bowls of salad and boiled potatoes, piles of well-done sausages, plus tomato sauce, salt, pepper, dressing, butter and bread circulated around the five brothers.

It was one of those rare weeknights when they were all home for dinner. Often Ryan worked late, and Marcus, the second-eldest of the five, went who-knows-where after he'd finished at the garage for the day. Luke's twin brother, Quinn, compared science experiment notes with his classmates, while Braydon, the youngest, volunteered at the animal shelter.

"So, how's school going?" asked Ryan from the head of the table, addressing no one in particular. He punched something into his cell phone and then pushed it aside.

Braydon, never one to miss an opportunity to join in a conversation, replied, "We've got camp at the end of next week."

"So soon in the new year? God, I'd forgotten." Ryan stuffed some sausage in his mouth. "What do you need to take?"

"The list is on the bench, remember?"

"Vaguely. I'll look at it after dinner. How about you, Quinn?"

"Mrs Sutherland thinks I have a good chance of getting on the science team, there's the maths comp in two weeks, and we're going up the Sounds to visit the salmon farm operation, I think at the end of the month. So it's all on." He waved his knife and fork around in the air as he spoke.

Luke dipped his head down. He was used to being overshadowed by his academically gifted brother.

There had never been any doubt about Quinn's career path. The straight-A student would be off to university next year to study for a Bachelor of Science.

Luke chomped into his second slice of bread. Eventually the questions would be directed his way. Would he be able to escape interrogation tonight? Frazzled from the heat of the day, he was too tired to think and the bread stuck to the roof of his mouth.

Marcus's cell phone buzzed and he tapped out a reply.

"Luke, how about you?" Ryan snapped.

Oh boy, there it goes. "It's going good."

"When's your first assignment due?"

"End of next week."

"What's it on?"

"It's a book review for English."

"What's the book?"

"*The Summer Now Ending.*"

"I remember reading that," said Marcus, still busy tapping. "It wasn't bad. Some good themes around following your own path despite what others may want for you."

"How long have you had the assignment for?" Ryan asked, drumming his fingers on the table.

"Since last week," Luke mumbled.

"Why do you have to leave everything to the last minute?"

"I didn't. I kind of forgot."

Ryan sighed. "You never change. It's always 'I forgot', or you lose track of time. You really need to smarten up."

Luke pushed his chair back, eager to leave, but Ryan hadn't finished.

"You don't have many chances left. This will be your final year at high school. Have you given any thought to what you're going to do at the end of the year? Where you want your life to go?" His drumming fingers speeded up.

Luke stared at his empty plate, his mind a blank. Too many questions, with too few answers.

He lifted his head in time to see Marcus, Quinn and Braydon shoot sideways looks at each other. How many times had they witnessed a full-blown argument between Ryan and himself? Luke didn't see eye to eye with Ryan, who relentlessly pressured him over his performance (or lack of) at school. Chalk and cheese.

"Hey," Marcus cut in. "I thought I'd go down to Haven River after dinner for a swim at the waterfall. You guys wanna come?"

"You bet," yelled Quinn.

"Yip," shouted Braydon.

It would be a great way to end a hot day. The gushing, spurting, sluicing force of the river could tear away his restlessness.

"I'm in," Luke said, passing a finger along the neck of his T-shirt, releasing the sticky material that clung to his chest.

"Quinn and Braydon can go. Luke, I want you to start that book tonight," Ryan said, the military-like command shooting out of him.

Luke glared at Ryan. He could sometimes be a right pain in the arse, playing the heavy hand because he thought Luke needed it.

Quinn, Marcus and Braydon darted about, gathering swimming shorts, towels and bags.

Luke poked his fork into a half-eaten sausage and brooded over Ryan's unfair order.

Braydon patted Luke's shoulder. "We'll take an extra swim for you."

"Are you coming, Ryan?" Marcus asked.

"Would love to, but I need to go over the work rosters for next week."

"You work too hard."

Ryan grimaced, but his attention was diverted as his cell phone rang.

The brothers bundled out the door.

"Be careful. Watch the railway line, and it's a school night." Ryan's voice was drowned by the slam of the front door and the brothers' banter.

With Ryan on the phone, Luke took the opportunity to escape. He hot-trotted upstairs to the bedroom he shared with Quinn.

Luke switched on the computer. While it kicked into life, he removed his books from his back pack and placed them on the desk. He didn't know why he'd a general reluctance to study. Something made it all too hard. It wasn't that he didn't like school - he did, particularly English. He loved to make up stories, but a barrier prevented him from getting the words out of his head. As he started to type he would forget how to spell a word. Sure, the spell-checker helped but he just couldn't leave spellchecking his work until the end. He needed to have the right word and have it spelt correctly. But by then the moment had passed and he'd lost the flow.

Luke picked up the *The Summer Now Ending* off the top of the book pile.

He threw the windows wide open and clambered onto his bed his head sinking into the comfortable softness of two pillows. He read the back cover of the book.

*Daniel Jenkins, has spent his whole life living in a sleepy, Australian outback town.*

*But that was about to change. To fulfil his parents' wishes and against what he wanted, Daniel prepares to leave the comfort of the familiar to embark on university study in a city of over four million people.*

*As the day draws closer for Daniel to leave his family, friends and the security he has always known he fights an overwhelming feeling of self-doubt and anxiety.*

*Will the city bear the opportunities waiting for him or will he be swallowed up in an uncaring world?*

*What effects will maintaining a long-distance relationship have on both himself and his childhood sweetheart, Melanie?*

*Daniel must face these fears on his journey to adulthood and carve out an identity for himself.*

Daniel sounded like him. Fear of the unknown. Luke swallowed hard. Just reading the words 'self-doubt' and 'anxiety' made his stomach churn.

He flipped the book over to the front. Dawn in the country. That special time when nature slowly comes to life. Fields that went on and on, separated by large trees or wire fencing. Wisps of fog hugging the ground. Luke could almost feel the slight foggy chill. In the middle of the photo long driveways spoked out of the main road which led to a scattering of old wooden houses. In the absence of animal life Luke imagined sheep baa-ing. The sun had awakened, casting peacefulness over the gold-tinged fields.

Luke opened the book to the first page. All was good until he got to page three. Then it happened. The words swam on the page, preventing him from focusing on them. Dizziness enveloped him and he stopped. This had happened for as long as he could remember. He wasn't sure why it happened and he'd never mentioned it to anyone. Maybe because no-one had ever shown much interest in what he did. His brothers were the more interesting people. Perhaps all he needed was glasses. Great. Another reason to make Ryan grumpy about more expenses, and another reason for his classmates to tease him.

He sighed and rubbed his sore eyes. He let the book drop to the floor. It just wasn't going to happen tonight.

His eyes travelled to the enormous poster on the wall. Three-quarters of it was taken up by the menacing black form of a tornado, which was whipping everything into its destructive path. In the foreground, standing with his back to the photographer was the award-winning journalist, Michael Sharp. Michael accompanied storm chasers in the notorious tornado alley in the US and reported on their quest to capture storm data that often put them in life-threatening situations. Michael was Luke's hero and he wanted to be just like him - to be a journalist reporting on storms and tornados would be the coolest job in the world. A job where he could write for a living and report on weather phenomena. He followed Michael's Facebook page and devoured everything the guy wrote - slowly.

Luke rummaged around in his desk for his journal. He turned over the worn, dog-eared and tatty pages, the familiar roughness reassuring against his hand. He would need to get a new one soon.

Pictures stuck randomly within the notebook stared back at him. Landscape scenes, the All Blacks, *The Matrix* movie stickers and cut outs of Eminem, Linkin' Park, Foo Fighters and Pearl Jam.

Luke had kept a journal since his folks died - something the counsellor had suggested might help him deal with his grief. It had been a source of comfort for him, even now four years on.

He could rely on his journal 100 per cent. It was always there, reassuring, and it never talked back to him.

Telling him he was no good.

To try harder.

Passing judgement.

He wrote most days. Sometimes it was just random lines; sometimes the words grew a life of their own and turned into poems.

He wrote what he felt.

What he thought he was.

What he wanted to be.

His journal was his best friend and he'd never shared it with anyone. Not even Quinn. When Quinn saw Luke writing in his journal he would good-naturedly tease him that he was "worshipping the altar".

But lately nothing had inspired him to write.

He popped the journal back in the drawer, logged onto the computer and idly browsed the internet. Should he search on *The*

*Summer Now Ending*? Someone might have posted a review of the book he could use. He discarded the idea; it would be dishonest and it didn't sit comfortably with him. He continued to browse ending up at his favourite websites, CNN and BBC, where he intently studied the journalism style.

***

Luke had lost track of time. He glanced at the clock - 9.35. Had he been surfing for that long? He yawned catching a glimpse of *The Summer Now Ending* on the desk, guilt snapping at him. He stripped and slumped into bed. What would he tell Ryan tomorrow when he was asked about the book? He grimaced and his chest tightened. A slight sweat broke out on his forehead. And it wasn't just from the heat.

***

Luke tossed and turned. Every minute seemed like an hour. The curtains billowed gently in the warm breeze.

Sleep eluded him – again. Most nights it would take him hours to get to sleep and he suffered for it the next day. Dry eye-balls and a heavy head made for tough concentration at school.

He teetered on the precipice of the sleep world. The poem he'd been composing floated around in his head. The words were almost there:

*Creamy sand and*

*Green-blue sea*

*Fields of golden grass.*

*Lakes, rivers, streams*

*Sharp-peak, snow clad mountains*

*Something, something, something...*

He jerked awake.

He tossed.

He turned.

He tossed back.

He rolled the other way.

He kicked the covers completely off the bed.

He glanced at the clock on the desk. The red lights glowed 11:00.

Stairs creaking, hushed whispers and muffled movements. His brothers were back.

Quinn tiptoed into the room and ruffled the sheets as he climbed into bed.

"I'm still awake," Luke whispered.

"It's way too hot to sleep."

"How was the river?"

"We went up to the watering hole where the water was clearer. The river was still murky and muddy from last week's storm. Big, old gnarly branches were floating downstream. Sorry you couldn't come."

Luke's breath came out in a force of exasperation.

Quinn turned over onto his stomach. "You know - I don't think Ryan means to get uptight about your school work. He just wants you to do well."

"Yeah, I know. I just wish he would lay off a bit. It's hard to compete against you. And Marcus. And Braydon."

A couple of minutes stretched past. Luke's mind was at full-tilt now and in the dark of the night when nothing made sense and the heat pressed on him with fingers that gripped tighter, a question he'd always had a fear of asking grew monster arms.

"Do you think I'm dumb?" Luke asked.

There was a long silence.

"Quinn?"

Was the answer one not even Quinn wanted to reveal?

"Quinn?"

From his twin brother's bed came the regular breathing of someone who had fallen into an easy sleep.

Luke stared up at the ceiling, glad in a way that he hadn't heard Quinn's response.

He peeked at the clock again. 11:20, taunted him.

He grabbed the nearest cushion off the floor and threw it at the clock.

The black night stretched out before him, each second, minute and hour trailing their feet.

# Chapter 2

After showering and putting on his school uniform, Luke ambled down to the kitchen, the sun streaming in promising another hot day.

Luke stifled a yawn, pulled a bowl out of the dishwasher and tipped in some cereal. Quinn handed him a glass of milk.

Luke peered into the lounge. "Ryan gone?"

"Up with the birds. He left about six."

Luke half-smiled. The day looked better already.

"Do you want to meet up for lunch?" he and Quinn asked in unison.

Quinn's grin reflected back Luke's. That twin thing of being one body, one mind. They weren't identical but each had short, straight brown hair, brown eyes and a slender build.

"Meet you outside the library." Quinn grabbed some fruit for his lunch. "I have study group. Braydon!" he yelled. "I'm leaving now."

Luke peeked through the window as Quinn and Braydon walked down the long driveway. The house hung in silence. The walls creaked contracting with the growing heat.

Luke ventured into the lounge, screwing up his nose at the empty glasses on the coffee table. Why couldn't people put their dirty dishes in the dishwasher? He passed the threadbare couch that held memories of the rough and tumble games the brothers used to play. He reached over to pick up the glasses and knocked over a photo frame. He snatched at it and missed as it fell onto the carpet. Luke bent down to retrieve it. The photo had fallen face up. His folks stared back at him. It had been taken five years ago, a year before the fire. Before they'd taken that rare weekend away, without the children, that had ended in tragedy.

Luke wiped his finger over the photo as if this small action could bring his mum and dad back to life, to have the family back together again.

The photo reflected the family's chaotic meal times. Seven people at the table created a lot of fun. Luke smiled. Happy times when the family was together sharing whatever it was that had been significant for them that day. The laughter, the good-natured teasing played around in his head. So different to their meal times now - if they could all be there and get through a meal without a phone going off, someone replying to a text or Ryan at his throat.

His mum, Carolyn, her hair tied back, a constant smile on her face revelling in the challenges of raising five boys. His dad, Tim, who loved the outdoors, often taking the boys away for the weekend on fishing and hunting trips. A steady, solid man keen to instil good old-fashioned values in his sons.

Tim had had little success at school and had worked all his life on farms. He'd never pressured Luke. "There's more to life than getting good grades and being top at something," he would often say.

Carolyn's eyebrows would rise at this regular comment. She wanted all her sons to do the best they could.

And where Luke failed academically, Ryan overcompensated. The family's star pupil, the model son. Top of his class in his last year of high school. A university education awaited him but all that changed when Carolyn and Tim died.

A lump formed in his throat. Hell, he missed his dad. Missed the close bond between them that had grown each year when both dad and son knew they understood each other. He was his father's son.

There was no way Tim would be hassling him the way Ryan did.

Staring at the photo would not bring his dad back. He'd Ryan to answer to now.

Splintery shivers ran up Luke's spine. A sixth sense on high alert emitting a warning that things between him and Ryan were about to be tested beyond anything they had ever come up against before.

# Chapter 3

Luke wandered down the main street. A few metres in front of him a female pulled a box off a jeep's passenger's seat.

She juggled the box, handbag, drink bottle and keys but the slight shift in weight sent the box crashing to the ground. The drink bottle hit the guttering and bounced under the jeep and the contents of her handbag fell out dispersing themselves everywhere. The bottom of the box gave way and books tumbled out.

"Crap!" she exclaimed, surveying the mess. She bent down to pick up her keys.

"Here, let me help," Luke said.

She glanced up while fumbling around on the footpath. "Thanks," she replied, diving to grab a tube of lip gloss before it rolled off the footpath and into the drain.

Luke picked up a couple of other lip glosses, a nail polish, a comb and tissues. He handed her the escapees. "I'll get the books."

"Thanks," she said again. "I was probably being over ambitious, as usual, trying to carry too much."

She put everything that had come out of the handbag back into it and recovered the drink bottle from under the jeep. Luke picked up the books.

"I think the box is broken," he stated, holding up the torn box.

She laughed, tossing her raven hair. Her green eyes sparkled and Luke's heart jumped. When had he ever been captivated by a woman's eyes?

"I'm going into The Book Vine." She nodded her head towards the town's only second-hand bookshop. "Come on in," she said, as she unlocked the front door. She quickly disarmed the security system. "Pop the books onto the counter."

She switched on the lights bringing the shop to life.

Luke breathed in the musty old aroma of used books.

"I'm Jamie,' she introduced herself.

"Luke."

His eyes flicked her once over. Her jeans went on forever. Her white T-shirt with red sequins spelt out USA and hugged her curvy chest. The sequins twinkled in the shop light as she moved, mesmerising him. She was about his age but there was something about her that suggested a maturity that had had to be learnt quickly.

"I'm on my way to school..." he said. How obvious. I'm in my school uniform.

"For such a small town, there seems to be rush hour traffic with everyone off to school, work, whatever, plus all the ferry traffic. I thought stopping off at the supermarket to grab some groceries would be an easy task but it has made me late. I hate being late. I need to make sure the shop opens on time at 9," Jamie said.

Luke glanced around his favourite shop. Every time he came in here a rush of anticipation and anxiety swept through him. The anticipation came from his love of being surrounded by books and magazines. Books with characters - good and bad, heroes and villains, children, teenagers, adults, wizards and even animals. A world of make believe where no one judged and you could escape into whatever world you wanted. He loved to spend time in here trawling through old copies of *Time* and *National Geographic*. Michael Sharp's articles often appeared in *National Geographic*. He would flick over to the contents page moving his long fingers down looking for something that Michael had written. Michael's last article had been on *Global Warming: Fact or Fiction*? Instead of Michael's name as the journalist, it was his own. Luke blinked again. But it wasn't his name, of course. But maybe one day... The anxiety grew from the desperation of wanting to read but when he did it would take him forever - a slow, painful process.

"Luke?" A clear, silvery voice came from a distance. "Luke?"

Luke jolted himself back to the present. "Sorry."

"You were miles away. I really must be boring you with all my chatter." Jamie laughed.

"No, no. I'd better be off to school though," he said, pointing towards the door. Being at school on time had dropped way down the list.

As he turned away, his eye caught a book resting on top of the counter. He picked it up. It was *The Summer Now Ending*.

"That's a great book," Jamie commented.

"Yeah, I know."

"You've read it then?"

"Yes." Whoa! That was a massive lie. He rubbed his eyes.

"What do you like about the book? I must have read it a million times; it's one of my favourites."

"Actually, I kind of like the photo on the cover," Luke replied, holding up the book.

"Yep. It's a great shot."

Luke shifted from side to side. What should he say next? Man, he was out of practice with this girl-talk thing. If the discussion pushed on it may head off on to something he wouldn't be able to contribute to. Now was a good time to quit while he was ahead.

"I'd better go," he said again.

"Thanks."

"No probs," Luke said, exiting the shop.

The high school was just another block away and within minutes Luke had zigzagged his way into the rowdy classroom just as the bell rang announcing period one.

Mr Bligh, his English teacher, didn't mess around jumping quickly into today's lesson.

"By now you should've started your book and aiming to be at least half-way through by Friday." Mr Bligh raised his voice above the various groans.

"It's too hot to read," called out Nigel.

"Yeah. They need to invent plastic books so we can read them in the pool."

"They have. They're called waterproof bath books for babies."

The class erupted in laughter.

"Regardless of how hot it is, half-way by Friday," Mr Bligh said. "OK. Moving on. Today's lesson will be on creative writing."

He handed out selections of landscapes and explained that this particular subject required them to discuss the writer's view of the scene through narrative, structure, figurative language or point of view.

Luke flicked through the photographs. One in particular caught his eye.

Two parallel rows of enormous trees lined the country road. Their leaves danced in the sunlight. Vivid colours of red, orange, yellow and gold with a contradiction of green leaves sprinkled with brown leaves already long dead. The scene burst in the throes of autumn and all its magnificent colour. A crumbling road separated the rows. Roots of trees protruded up through the road forming large and uneven humps. Years of pounding rain, hot baking sun and country traffic had worn the asphalt down creating big potholes. The white centre markings had long since disappeared.

Something drew him in. The road was devoid of traffic. Where did the road go? Maybe he could write from the point of view of what the road stood for metaphorically. A journey from the point of view... something about the road less travelled? Maybe he could turn that around and make it about the same road travelled too many times and making the same mistakes. Or the empty road mirroring his own life – empty road, empty life, going where? Going nowhere.

Mr Bligh gave out further instructions. Something about having the remainder of the class to work on it, when it was due and the word limit.

He already had the story written in his head.

Luke focused back on his surroundings. His classmates were looking through the scenes generally in pairs, whispering agreement at which landscape they would choose and from which point of view they would write. He preferred to work by himself. It was less confusing and it allowed him to get his thoughts into perspective in his own time.

He pulled his refill pad out of his bag and opened it to a fresh page, his pen poised away from him and almost parallel with the paper. The first six words flew across the page but then he stumbled on how to spell the next word. The word, tractor, stared back at him. Tractor. E – r or o – r? Something wasn't right. Was the word spelt correctly? A letter looked back-to-front. Or was it? Now he'd lost the flow of his thinking, everything evaporating from his head.

Luke scratched his head raking his nails back and forth on his scalp. He jumped at the clanging of the bell. He bit his nail and stared at the almost blank page. Had it taken 20 minutes to write four lines?

Luke threw his pad into his bag sighing at the prospect of a weekend ahead that would be filled with playing catch-up on school assignments.

And it was only the third week of the new school year.

# Chapter 4

Luke forced open one eye and dangled a leg over the side of the bed. Saturday morning. No school. Sunlight shone on the drapes and the late morning heat laid warm waves across his leg.

He raised his head and squinted at the empty and unmade bed on the other side of the room. Quinn had gone. He beat Luke out of bed every day.

The whir of the vacuum cleaner and the hum of the washing machine drifted upstairs.

What to do today? He stretched like a cat, pushing to the back of his mind the number of assignments he needed to work on. Maybe later. His mind diverted to a brief vision of green eyes and raven hair.

He could go downtown and hang around for a while. Take *The Summer Now Ending*. Find a quiet spot on the beach and read.

Once he'd had his shower, made his bed and straightened his side of the room he strolled downstairs. Ryan was pushing the vacuum cleaner around like it was some wild beast that he had to tame. Luke changed his mind about having breakfast. He would grab something in town. That way he would avoid Ryan.

Luke was almost out the door when Ryan shouted, "Luke-"

"Later."

The front door banged shut cutting off a flimsy connection.

He strolled into town, breathing in the solidness of the salty, seaweedy air. He passed the bank, the games arcade, the dairy, tattoo studio, various clothes stores and tourist operators and without planning on it, walked into The Book Vine.

Luke visited the large, old, wooden shop at least once a week. Chairs stood regally on the uncarpeted floors complementing the total olde worlde air of the shop. A couple of worn, brown couches hid towards the rear like they were almost embarrassed to be there. He passed the children's, self-help, history, young adult, chick lit, sci-fi, true crime books, and the fantasy/paranormal section, the latest fad popular with the girls. The books turned over quickly as tourists exchanged their well-read and well-travelled reads for another. He browsed amongst the crime and thriller section. He'd read a couple of James Patterson and Dean Koontz's books. It would take awhile to read them but the fast-moving plot, short chapters and easy dialogue kept him engaged.

He'd the shop to himself. The coolness of the beach or river had lured people away providing escape from the relentless heat of the last week. Two fans droned in the background.

Luke thumbed the spines of the crime books. He picked one up and flipped it over to the back.

"Can I help?" a voice said beside him. "Oh it's you. Luke? That's right?"

"Hi, Jamie."

"Are you stalking me?" She smiled, tilting her head and revealing an ear with two gold studs.

"No, no," he stammered, heat rising in his cheeks.

"Only joking." Her smile hinted at mischief. "You don't need to check up on me. I've managed to get through this morning without any dramas."

"That's good."

"It's been slow." She switched off one of the fans. "I think everyone has gone to the beach. Is the weather always as good as this?"

"Generally we have a decent summer but we do seem to be experiencing a bit of a heat wave at the mo."

Jamie bent over to turn off the other fan. His eyes passed over her white pedal pushers, which outlined her small, defined butt. His chest contracted and he quickly looked away.

"I'm closing up now." Jamie turned around. "Did you want to buy anything?"

"Just browsing."

"I thought I would have a quick lunch at the café next door. Would you like to join me?"

Luke stared at the shelf of books, his tongue jamming in his mouth.

"I'll buy you a drink," said Jamie.

He fiddled with the binding of a book.

"I'll pay. For helping me yesterday," she persisted.

Luke hesitated.

"Come on. I don't bite."

Luke flicked her a tight smile. "Sure. That would be good."

"I'll just finish up here."

She scurried around the shop switching off lights and closing doors.

"OK," she said. "That's it." She grabbed her bag and took a last look around the shop. After engaging the security system, they exited the shop together.

"How about we get something from in here?" Jamie suggested as she peered through the Spik and Span's windows.

"There's a nicer one, Café Salt, just a bit further down."

"I'm still figuring out where the good places are to eat."

They continued down the street. Luke wanted to stay away from The Spik and Span. The food was OK and therefore cheap so it attracted the high school students. He didn't want anyone to see him with Jamie – only to avoid the inevitable teasing he would receive from his classmates because he was out with a girl.

Luke and Jamie entered Café Salt to the beat of lounge music. The tables were set in alcoves providing diners privacy.

Jamie ordered a chicken roll and an OJ. "What would you like?"

He would keep things simple. "Same as you."

Jamie placed the order. Like the bookshop, it was unusually quiet for a Saturday with only one other couple and three backpackers eating. Jamie followed Luke to an alcove towards the back.

"This café has a nice feel about it," Jamie said, looking around her.

"It's my favourite. The coffee is really good." His leg jiggled up and down in time with the music.

'I haven't..."

"Where do you..."

They both started at the same time and then laughed, easing the moment.

"I haven't seen you around town before," Luke started again.

"No. I'm a newbie. I'm looking after the shop for three months while Aunt Yvette and Uncle Stuart and their two kids travel around Australia. I've done a lot of helping out in second-hand bookshops as holiday jobs so that's why I jumped at the chance to look after the shop."

"I know your Aunt Yvette well. She's cool. I'm a regular shopper at The Book Vine. Actually I tend to browse more than shop but I really like books."

"Me too," Jamie replied. "Being surrounded by books all day, what more could anyone want?" Her eyes widened and the green eyes glowed.

Luke nodded in agreement, pumped to be having a conversation with someone who loved books as much as he did. "Where are you from?" he asked.

"Wellington. I finished school at the end of last year and I'm earning some cash before I go overseas later on this year."

"Doing the big OE?"

"Mmm." She nodded. "I'm volunteering for a year to work at an orphanage in South Africa."

"You don't get paid for it?"

"No. Have you heard of the concept of paying it forward?"

Luke shook his head.

"It's about helping others in some way to pay back what help others have given you in the past."

Luke caught a waver in Jamie's voice.

The waitress appeared with their food and drink rescuing Luke from the awkward situation.

"It's great that you know what you're doing," Luke said. "I wish it was that clear for me. I'm in my last year of school but I'm not sure what I'll do when I leave."

"Have you lived in Haven River all your life?

"Yeah. We live just down Resolution Bay Road. Huge tree outside just before you hit the railway line."

"We?" Jamie asked, her composure recovered.

"I've four brothers."

"Gosh. I'm an only child. I can't imagine having that many siblings."

"With four brothers there's always someone to hang out with. We're a tight unit but it seems as though we're gradually pulling away from each other." When had this small change started creeping in? They all had different priorities now, leading them off on to separate paths.

"What do your folks do?" Jamie asked. She picked up a serviette and dabbed her mouth.

"They died in a house fire four years ago." Luke gulped. It never got any easier to say.

"Oh!" Jamie exclaimed, a distant look in her eyes. "I'm sorry. That must be hard."

"Yeah," Luke said. "It was pretty devastating. We stayed with our grandparents for awhile but they died within a year. Ryan, our older brother who's a vineyard supervisor, became our legal guardian. He has kept us all together - otherwise we would've ended up in separate foster homes." He swigged at his OJ.

"That's a pretty cool thing for Ryan to do."

"He's given up a lot and has worked really hard to ensure we don't go without."

"Are your other brothers younger than you?"

"Marcus is 18. Braydon is 13. And Quinn is my twin brother."

"Ah, so there are two of you." Jamie's mouth turned up in a wicked smile.

"We're not identical and we're quite different. He's the brainy one."

"I bet you're brainy too," Jamie said. "You obviously read a lot."

"Surprisingly I'm not that good at reading. I struggle with it." Luke shifted in his chair. This was something he'd never mentioned before to anyone. "My grades aren't great. And Ryan and I have differences over what I should be doing or thinking of doing." Luke clenched his glass.

"What do you mean?"

Luke would never forget the heated discussion he'd had with Ryan last year when both of them were discussing his final-school-year subjects. They agreed on English, Computing/Digital Technologies and History but Ryan insisted Luke also take Algebra, and Business Studies. Luke's marks reflected he was abysmal at algebra. He detested the sight of figures. Surely it wasn't right that he still needed to count on his fingers and couldn't work out sequenced information? It had all got harder and harder. He always managed to scrape through but this year the stakes would be higher.

He briefly explained this to Jamie adding, "Ryan also thought taking Business Studies would give me a solid grounding for any job when I leave school. I can see his point but the subject bores me to death and I just can't see myself working in retail, banking, commerce, IT. I wanted to do something more like me like Media Studies – creative writing, media – newspapers, TV, internet. But Ryan didn't see it that way. It wasn't practical enough for him. He's intolerant of subjects like art. He calls them 'fluff'."

Luke relaxed his grip on the glass. At long last someone was listening to him. This added conviction to the direction he wanted to take.

"That's a toughie," Jamie said.

"I find it really hard to get excited about business. It's just not me." Luke sighed. "I should probably go. I need to read some more of *The Summer Now Ending*."

Luke pulled the book out of his bag and placed it on the table. "That's my task for this afternoon."

"Where are you up to?"

"I'm halfway."

"Oh then, you'll be up to the interesting part where Daniel meets a girl he's quite attracted to but then he starts to feel guilty about Melanie. What do you think he should do? And then there's the complicating issue of his lecturer, Sally. That's becoming interesting. What do you think is going to happen there?"

36

Silence. Jamie raised her eyebrows as she waited for an answer.

He'd wanted to impress Jamie but now he'd dug a hole for himself. Why on earth had he said he was halfway through the book?

"Um, I forgot there's something I need to do," Luke replied, getting up in a rush. "Thanks for the lunch. I'll see you around."

Luke tugged on his backpack and hurried out of the cafe.

*** 

Under the huge tree in the front garden, Luke raised an axe and swung it down on the block of wood. Rivulets of sweat ran down his bare chest. He turned his head when a car door slammed.

"Hi again," Luke said.

"Hi." Jamie cast her eyes downwards.

Luke placed the axe carefully on the ground. He wiped a towel over his chest and threw a T-shirt over his head.

"Are you stalking *me*?" he asked.

Jamie laughed. "Very funny. I think you forgot something." She handed him the book.

"Oh yeah." He glanced sideways, avoiding her eyes. "I realised when I left the cafe that I'd left it behind but when I went back you and the book had gone." A burning in his cheeks as he lied again. He hadn't gone back to the shop. He just didn't want to talk about the book. He hadn't thought that she would make the effort to drop it off

37

to him. "I came home and decided why not torment myself in the heat by chopping wood."

"I knew how much you wanted to read it. And as you are up to such an exciting place it wasn't out of my way to drop it off."

"I'm going to get a drink. Would you like one?"

"Sure. I seem to be drinking constantly in this hot weather."

As they walked towards the house, there was a rustling in the border hedge and a long haired tortoiseshell cat emerged.

"Meet Trixibelle." Luke introduced the cat to Jamie. "Hey, Trix." Luke put out his hand. Trixibelle sniffed him and then weaved her way between his legs, purring flat out. He bent down to stroke her fur, matted from a lazy day of lying in the dirt in the shade. He pulled out a couple of biddi-biddis.

"Such a friendly cat," Jamie said.

"Probably because she's hungry. Come inside."

Luke opened the door for Jamie. Ryan and Braydon were deep in conversation.

"How goes it with the animals?" Ryan asked Braydon as he placed an empty glass in the dishwasher.

Braydon gulped down the last of his drink. "Good," he replied, wiping his mouth on the back of his hand. "Some abandoned kittens came in over the weekend. I helped de-flea them."

"Don't get any bright ideas about bringing home any kittens," Ryan warned.

Braydon's love of animals had meant various strays becoming temporary or permanent residents of the Conway household over the years. Trixibelle was Braydon's pride and joy, since he'd raised her from a kitten.

"I know. I know." Braydon sighed. "The shelter is running a course on natural herbal therapies for animals next Saturday. Can I go?"

"Maybe. I'll be increasing my hours at the end of the week so I might be working Saturday. I won't be able to take you there."

Braydon pouted and cast his eyes downward.

"But we'll see what we can work out," Ryan said.

Ryan and Braydon looked up.

"You've brought a friend home," Ryan stated.

"Yes," Luke replied.

"She's a girl."

'I'm aware of that."

"Luke never brings girls home," Braydon added.

Luke shuffled his feet. "This is Jamie."

"Hi," said Braydon.

"Pleased to meet you." Ryan shot out his hand.

"Same," Jamie responded, shaking his hand. "Luke mentioned you."

Suspicion simmered in Ryan's eyes. "I hope it was all good."

"Nothing but."

Ryan beamed. "Yep. I'm the best brother in the world." Ryan playfully swiped a hand across the top of Luke's head. Luke returned the grin.

As Braydon left the kitchen and detoured into the lounge, the front door banged shut again and Marcus sauntered in. The apprentice mechanic had smears of grease on his face, and well-worked overalls.

"Hey brother," he said, speaking to no one in particular.

"Hey brother," Ryan and Luke said at the same time using the traditional family greeting.

"Home so early? Take off your overalls before you get grease and dirt all over the place," Ryan said.

"Yes, mum." Marcus unzipped the front of his overalls and grappled to pull a muscular arm out of its sleeve. Underneath he wore a T-shirt and board shorts. His left arm had a tattoo of a burning house and his right arm bore his brothers' birthdates.

Marcus caught another presence out of the corner of his eye.

"Oh hi," he said, roaming his eyes over Jamie.

"This is Jamie," said Luke.

"She's a girl," Marcus replied.

"Yes."

"You never bring girls home."

Luke rolled his eyes. "Call the newspapers. They may want to know." Why was he repeating the same lines of a minute ago?

Luke, keen to exit the kitchen, took a bottle of lemonade from the fridge and poured the sparkling liquid into two glasses. He plopped ice cubes into the drinks, which fizzed and popped. He handed a glass to Jamie.

Luke gulped down the sweet and citrusy liquid.

Jamie drained her drink in one go. "I'd better be going. Thanks for the drink."

"How are you going with your book report?" Ryan turned to face Luke.

"Getting there," Luke said.

"That's a bit vague." Ryan's chin lifted upwards. "What chapter are you up to? What's the assignment? When's it due again?"

Luke, disconcerted by the quick-fire questions, raised his voice. "Really, Ryan. Quit hassling me. I'm onto it."

"Well maybe if you'd got up earlier this morning instead of lazing in bed until 11 you might be further ahead."

"I didn't sleep well last night," Luke mumbled.

"Excuses. That's all they are. 'I was late.' 'I didn't sleep well.' 'I'll do it later.' 'When I'm in the mood.' It doesn't achieve anything, Luke."

"Give me a break. I said I was getting there. Why can't you leave it at that?"

"This attitude isn't helping. You'll have to stay on another year at school if you don't pull your finger out." Ryan slapped the dish-cloth down on the bench.

"I've offered to help Luke with his book report," Jamie said. "It was part of our curriculum last year."

"You're not in Luke's class?" queried Ryan.

"No. I finished school last year. I'm managing The Book Vine at the moment."

"Well, he needs all the help he can get." Ryan snatched up a tea towel from the rail.

Jamie stared at Ryan as she let the careless comment slide.

"Come on, Jamie." Luke glared at Ryan and turned towards the stairs that led up to the second floor.

Jamie followed Luke. At the top, the second floor branched out into three bedrooms and a bathroom. Luke opened the door to the first bedroom. The air hit them like they were walking into a hot furnace. The window must've blown shut after he left this morning. He shut the door and then threw the window back open.

Luke cast a weary eye around the room and sighed. "I'm sorry for the mess. I share this room with Quinn."

Both sides of the room were relatively identical with two double beds and a set of drawers. Two desks separated the room one of which had a computer on it.

"Is Quinn's the messy side?"

Luke nodded.

Quinn's side of the room had clothes, clean and dirty, strewn everywhere. Books, papers, food wrappings and CDs, covered the unmade bed. Posters of sciencey things draped crookedly across the wall.

Luke's bed was neatly made, books in orderly piles on the desk, CDs and DVDS in alphabetical order. Clothes hung neatly in the half-open wardrobe. *The Matrix* movie poster hung next to Michael Sharp.

Jamie wandered over to Quinn's side. On top of the drawer was a half-completed science experiment.

"What's in the test tubes?" she asked, peering into them.

"Not sure but I hope they're not going to explode any time soon."

The breeze had now increased in the room and papers started blowing off desks.

"Whoa!" said Luke, trying to catch the dancing papers.

Downstairs the front door slammed. Feet pounded on the stairs and the bedroom door flew open. The extra draught in the room created a whirlwind effect and more stuff left their spots to find new places to explore.

"Hey! Can you not make such a grand entrance?" Luke greeted Quinn.

"Cool," replied Quinn. Everything whirled and swirled. "It's like a witches' cauldron." Quinn threw his bag onto the floor.

Luke shut the door again while Quinn brought the window-latch back a fraction and the whirlwind subsided.

Quinn turned around and jumped when he saw Jamie staring back at him.

"Oh," he said. "It's a girl."

"Man, anybody would think this was a weird event in my life."

"It is," Quinn agreed. "I didn't even know you had a girlfriend. How could I not know?"

"She's not my girlfriend. We just met yesterday." Luke scratched his arm.

"And yet, you've managed to get her into our bedroom already."

"Quinn!"

"I'm only teasing. Loosen up. You take yourself too seriously." Quinn turned towards Jamie and introduced himself.

"You know. It wouldn't take much to clean up your side of the room - again," Luke said, as he turned over papers in his hand. Were they his or Quinn's?

"Well, I could, but you know it would be a waste of time," he replied, peering into his test tubes.

Luke divided the misplaced papers into three piles – his, Quinn's and what appeared to be rubbish.

"Anyway, I'm off again. Just needed to grab a few things." Quinn rustled around in his wardrobe. "A couple of guys discovered some dead possums so we're going to dissect them."

Luke screwed up his nose. "Right-o." Not his idea of how to spend a Saturday afternoon.

"Nice to meet you," Quinn said to Jamie as he left.

"Welcome to the Conway household. As you can tell, we're a bit off." Luke shrugged. What else could he say about his brothers' behaviours?

"Probably no more off than any other family," Jamie replied.

"Thanks for helping me out with that sticky situation with Ryan."

"No probs." Jamie smiled. "I'm happy to lend a hand."

Luke's mouth fell open. "Really? What, now?" Why would anyone give up their time to help him?

"Sounds good," she said. "Where do we start?"

He paused for a moment. "I know I have to work on the book report but there's an essay due on Wednesday. Maybe we could start there."

"Sure." Jamie sat down at the computer. "I just need some paper. Can I use this?"

"No, no." Luke grabbed at the note pad on the desk at the same time as Jamie. "Please don't read that."

"You write poetry?" Jamie said, as she studied the writing.

"It isn't very good." Luke snatched the note pad out of her hand. He wanted her to read his poetry but what would she think of the repetitions, additions, reversed letters and the incorrectly spelt words? If Jamie sees my writing she'll think I'm a moron. He bit at a fingernail. Early classroom memories of a metal ruler whacking across his hands for taking too long to write invaded his mind.

"I'm sorry. I didn't mean to pry."

"No, it's OK," Luke said, regretting his quick retort.

Luke wheeled another chair over towards the desk.

"OK. So what's the assignment about?" Jamie asked, looking at Luke.

Tingles ran up Luke's spine as he fell into her green eyes, eyes that drew him in and filled the room. He looked away unable to hold her gaze any longer. He cleared his throat and explained the essay assignment and his halting attempts as he struggled to put down on paper the words in his head. "I know what I want to say but I just can't get it written down. How about I dictate to you my ideas and you type."

Over the next two hours Luke and Jamie worked together to complete the essay assignment.

Jamie could type fast and had no problems keeping up with him. She even made some suggestions around structure and composition but the ideas and words belonged to Luke.

"Gosh. It's 3 o'clock," said Jamie, as she let out a gasp of air and rubbed her eyes and arms. "That time has flown by."

"I'm exhausted!" Luke laughed. "That would've taken me forever if it wasn't for your help. Thank you."

Luke couldn't believe how easy it had been to just get his ideas out without worrying about spelling and whether the words looked right. Whether Jamie would stare at the way he held his pen. The minutes had flown by as he dictated stuff to her and her fingers had flown across the keyboard. His first English assignment done and dusted.

"It was a good way to spend a Saturday afternoon." Jamie got up from the chair. "I've been sitting for too long," she moaned, stretching her back. "How about you print off a copy to edit 'cos I'm sure you will want to make some finishing touches. And print out an extra copy too."

"What's the extra one for?" Luke asked, popping some paper into the printer.

"You'll see."

Luke stapled the two copies and handed one to Jamie.

"I should go," she said.

Don't go. Could she hear his silent words?

Jamie hesitated a moment but made towards the door.

Together they walked downstairs and into the dining room.

Ryan sat at the table studying various papers and rubbing his forehead. His brow furrowed, creating deeper lines than you'd expect for someone his age. Luke moved closer; they were bills. Electricity, phone, car insurance, Braydon's camp fees, Quinn's science trip, the repair bill for the fridge.

Ryan manoeuvred the papers into one pile. Someone else wanting to hide something.

"Have a read of this," Jamie said placing Luke's work down on the table. "One assignment. Done. Not a big deal." She looked Ryan in the eye inviting a challenge then she turned and walked out the front door, not waiting for a response.

Luke half-grinned. Jamie wasn't afraid to stand up to Ryan. She had guts. And that was something he admired.

# Chapter 5

Luke sighed in relief as he handed in his essay on Monday. That was one weight off his shoulders. But he was nowhere near quarter through *The Summer Now Ending.*

Today's lesson would be on the book. Mr Bligh handed out a series of questions to get them thinking about the book's issues.

"OK. Pair up and get some discussion going on the themes," Mr Bligh said.

In the noisy hubbub, as chairs scraped back, people drifted into pairs – long established cliques, boy/girl couples, girl friends, mates.

Luke stood up, holding the sheet of questions close to his chest. How was he going to discuss themes when he hadn't even got past Chapter 2? He thumbed through the book. Half-way was Chapter 10.

"Want to buddy up?"

"Hey, Caitlin. Sure. How's things?" He pulled out a chair as Caitlin, flicking her blonde hair off her shoulders, sat down beside him.

Luke had gone to the same kindergarten as Caitlin and living in a town of only 20,000 people, like so many of his classmates, they had continued on through primary and high school together. He liked Caitlin. She was mature and not like the other girls her age. The ones who giggled non-stop and flirted with guys, even the male teachers.

"How was your summer?" she asked, turning to the first page.

"Good. I didn't see you much."

"No, I went up to Waiheke Island to stay with my dad and pesky half-brothers."

"How'd that go?"

"Not too bad. Better than I thought," Caitlin said, her pale blue eyes drifting. "Last year of high school."

"Yeah, yeah, yeah." His leg jiggled up and down. The more he talked, the more the conversation would stay off the book.

"Can't wait. My Mum said I can go to tech next year to do a hairdressing and beauty therapy qual – finally! I thought she'd never say yes."

"That's good." And what did the future hold for him exactly?

"So what kind of themes have you found so far?" Caitlin asked, opening the book.

"Umm, well..."

Andrew, who was sitting behind Caitlin, burst out laughing and rammed his chair up against her back.

"Hey!" She turned around and frowned.

"Sorry, Caitlin," Andrew said.

With Caitlin's attention diverted, Luke pulled the bookmark out of Chapter 2 and shoved it further into the book. Hadn't Jamie mentioned a growing relationship between Sally and Daniel? Maybe a theme was around Daniel feeling disloyal to Melanie.

"Jerk," Caitlin muttered, turning back around.

"One of the themes might be loyalty," Luke said.

"I so agree," Caitlin replied, immediately rattling off an argument around the virtues of loyalty.

Luke let her ramble jotting down a few notes – this was good information to use for the final book report.

After school he walked into town, glad to be escaping the prickly, dry heat of the classroom. With every step he took away from school the more the tension trickled out of his shoulders. Walking gave him time to think, to let his mind settle into one place. To quieten a brain that struggled against something. An opportunity to play with the words to a poem that was flitting around in his head. Sometimes Andrew and his mates would pull up to the curb and harass him. They hassled him for being slow, for being a dummy. *Whack, whack, whack – the metal ruler thumped across his hands.*

He always turned a blind eye and ear to the teasing. Responding back wouldn't change anything.

No sign of Andrew and his annoying mates. Today he would be left alone. Maybe the bright sunny day appealed to them to try new bait.

Luke walked into The Book Vine and hung back while Jamie finished serving a customer.

A woman tugged a book off a shelf, flicked through the pages, stopped at one and paused while she read. Would she buy the book? Would the passage she was reading capture her interest enough for her to want to find out more?

"Just to let you know, I handed in the essay," Luke said, as the customer walked away.

"Good for you." Jamie smiled at him while writing up price stickers. "I'm sure you'll get good marks. How's the report going?"

"Actually that's what I've come in to ask you. I wondered if... maybe... could you... would you be able-."

"Luke, just spit it out!"

"Well, would you be able to give me a hand with the book report?" He twiddled with the tassel on his backpack.

"Of course." Jamie strolled out behind the counter. "When do you want to start?"

"I kind of have a deadline so how about this afternoon?"

"Sure. How about you help me with some shelves I need moved and then we can start when I shut the shop at 4.30?"

Luke hummed while he relocated the shelves and when the last customer left and Jamie had put up the 'Closed' sign, they settled down to work.

"I have a confession. I'm only up to Chapter 2," Luke said, looking down at the book. It was time to come clean. "I'm a slow reader. I think it would be quicker for you to read to me."

"Sure thing," said Jamie.

The only place where the two of them could work was on the couch. Luke settled into one corner and Jamie sat beside him, keeping a polite distance.

Over the next hour, Jamie read Chapters 3 and 4 while Luke made notes. Once again he couldn't believe how quickly they were making progress. He'd completely lost track of time until Jamie pointed out that it was 5.30.

"I should be heading home," Luke said. "Thanks for your help."

"No worries." Jamie smiled.

"Would you like me to walk you home?" It was a small gesture to repay her for her time.

"Thanks for the offer but I think I can manage. I live just around the corner."

"That's OK. I don't mind."

"All right. If you insist," Jamie said. A sly grin crept across her face.

Jamie went through the regular ritual of locking up the shop and turning on the security system.

As they left the shop together, Jamie pointed in the direction they needed to go. They walked past the bank, the dairy, the café and around the corner until Jamie promptly stopped.

"This is it. This is where I live." She gestured to a flat that was offset from the street and directly behind The Book Vine.

Luke hung his head and looked at her sideways. "You're right. You do live literally around the corner."

"Told you!" The musical lilt in Jamie's laugh sent tingles down his spine. "I think I would've been quite safe in the distance I had to go."

"Can't you get to the flat from inside the shop?"

"Not at the moment. Long story. I'll tell you another day."

The question of same time, same place tomorrow hung in the air.

Maybe Jamie thinks she's given up enough of her time. Luke kicked a stone into the gutter.

Jamie spoke first. "Do you want to pop by tomorrow?"

"Sure." Luke breathed easier. She was just as keen as he was.

When Luke arrived back at the house, Ryan had dinner underway.

"Where have you been?" Ryan asked before Luke was barely in the room.

"Working on the book report."

Marcus chomped away on a hunk of bread. "Sure you weren't hanging out with your girlfriend?" he jibed.

"She's not my girlfriend and no I wasn't hanging out with her."

"Didn't I see you and Jamie walking down the main street 10 minutes ago?" Marcus asked.

Before Luke had a chance to answer Ryan interjected. "It would be better use of your time if you concentrated on your school-work and try and be prompt for dinner. I've enough worries without having to wonder where everyone is."

Ryan plonked two chipped plates down on the bench. "You and I need to have a chat about things." He pointed a finger at Luke. "I've got to go back to work. I'll see you guys later."

"Thanks Marcus." Luke eyeballed him.

"Hey, if I was you I'd be spending as much time as I could with Jamie. She's a real looker."

"Well, just stay out of it." Luke shot Marcus a warning look but as Jamie had received the thumbs-up from Marcus he bit his tongue to prevent him from saying anything more.

That evening as Luke surfed his favourite websites, his eye caught an advertisement.

### Journalism Scholarship

*The National Association of Journalism (NAJ) is seeking entries for the 5th Annual Journalism Scholarship.*

*NAJ will award scholarships to three secondary school students who display good academic achievement in creative writing and would like to pursue a career in journalism.*

*Scholarships cover the cost of tuition fees and accommodation for the first years' study in the National Diploma in Journalism.*

*Applicants are invited to submit a piece of work for consideration.*

*Please fill in the attached form and submit your application by 30 March.*

*For more information contact susan.meyer@naj.co.nz*

Luke stared at the screen, his pulse racing. Despite his struggle with reading and writing, his interest lay in books, magazines, creative writing, turning his hand to the odd piece of poetry. The idea of applying for a journalism scholarship fascinated him. But his initial sense of clarity faded as he contemplated Ryan's reaction. Ryan would never go for it, his objections already ringing loud in his ears.

Was journalism any less worthy than Quinn and his brilliant scientific mind or Marcus and his awesome mechanical ability? Even Ryan's encouragement of Braydon's interest in animals and budding veterinarian career eclipsed Luke's willingness to share his creative work with his older brother. He lingered in his brothers' shadows, a point to prove out of reach. And he wasn't academically worthy. Who was he kidding? He couldn't even finish an assignment, even on a subject he loved so much, without help from Jamie. Luke's eyes diverted to the Michael Sharp poster. It was too hard.

He printed off the advertisement and left it on top of the desk.

Just maybe…

# Chapter 6

Mr Bligh beckoned to Luke as he went to leave English class on Tuesday. Andrew and Zack made a big deal out of it, taunting and mocking him as they left the classroom.

Luke's facial muscles tensed.

"Just ignore them," Mr Bligh said.

Luke focused his attention back on Mr Bligh.

"I've been marking the essays," Mr Bligh started.

Luke waited. He hung his head and tapped the edge of the desk. What had he done wrong now? He didn't want to give Ryan any extra reason to bug him.

"What did you think of your essay?"

"I thought about it and spent a lot of time on it. I liked the picture and the idea of where the empty road might be going." Was this what Mr Bligh wanted to hear? He couldn't read his face and he faltered. "But I'm not sure I interpreted it all that well."

Mr Bligh flicked through the essays. "Now where's yours? Ahh – here."

Luke swallowed hard as Mr Bligh handed him his essay. The mark at the top of the page couldn't be true. The A+ winked back at him.

"Well done. You've produced excellent work," Mr Bligh said.

"Are you sure?" Luke shook his head.

"Absolutely. You have some real talent Luke. With focus and commitment you could develop it a lot more."

"Wow! Gee, thanks." Lightness swept over his chest. Jamie had thought his work was good and Mr Bligh had just confirmed it.

"I look forward to having you in my class this year."

"Thanks," Luke said again. He needed to share this with Jamie and after school he ran to The Book Vine. He almost knocked over two customers in his excitement to get in the door.

"Whoa! Hurricane. Where's the fire?" Jamie teased.

Luke showed her the mark.

"That's fantastic! We should frame it and pin it on the wall," she said.

That afternoon Luke and Jamie continued to work on *The Summer Now Ending*. The elation of the perfect essay mark buoyed Luke's enthusiasm as they debated issues and themes arising in the book.

By Thursday, after Jamie had shut up shop, they had fallen into a routine of spending an hour working through the book report. What started out at the beginning of the week of finishing by half-five gradually crept up to 6 pm. (He didn't worry that he had to be home by a certain time as Ryan was working extended shifts at the vineyard.

Dinners had already been prepared earlier on in the day and the guys just had to cook the veggies.) Afterwards Luke would then 'walk' Jamie to her flat and he would scoot on home riding on a wave of assurance - not only about his progress in English but how much he enjoyed spending time with Jamie. Amongst serious discussion they laughed. They talked over the top of one another as each spurred the other on with their ideas. He was discovering more about Jamie as each day passed. She liked to jog and dabbled in making her own clothes.

"So, what is it about books that you love?" asked Jamie.

"Everything. What's not to love? It's losing yourself in someone else's world, being transported to another time space. That feeling you get when you pick up a book, and by the time you've got to the tenth page you know that the book is going to be something special." Luke grinned

"It's not only the story but the words. Some authors have this amazing ability to write so poetically – poetry in motion. All you want to do is shut out the world and lose yourself completely in the words."

"Who writes like that?"

"I love Marcus Zusak. You know, *The Book Thief. When Dogs Cry.*"

"Yeah, yeah, yeah. What about *The Perks of Being a Wallflower?*"

"I love that book. So funny, sad too," Jamie said, her eyes reflecting the instant change of opposite emotions.

"Those are the books that when you've finished you just want to sit there and relive it all again. In fact, there've been a couple of books that when I've finished I've turned to the front and started all over again. You feel like you've lived the lives of the characters – felt their anguish, their wins and suffered with them through their low points. And feeling absolutely exhausted at the end of the story. And if there's a sequel, wanting to rush out to get the book." A throaty laugh escaped from Luke's mouth.

"And if there's no sequel, write one!"

"How did you get into books?"

"I think it's hereditary. My grandmother was a great reader and always reading. I think I was born with a book in my hand," said Jamie.

"I feel the best when I'm surrounded by books. I love the smell of them, the smell of paper and ink. There was a bookshop I went into once where one of the staff caught me sniffing a book. She insisted that if I sniffed the book I had to buy it!"

Jamie sighed. "I can lose myself for hours in a bookshop. Time just seems to stand still and I want to buy them all and read them all at once."

"I sometimes worry that one day all the stories will've been written and there'll be nothing left to write, or worse read."

"I worry I'll die before I've read everything." A statement that started out as frivolous was set to be shadowed by a solemnness drifting down from above.

"Is there a picture in your mind of what heaven looks like?" Luke asked, lowering his voice and chasing the melancholy moment away.

"Mmm. Heaven is a massive library. There will be walls and walls of books ad infinitum. You will need a ladder to get to the ones on the very top shelves. Like the libraries you see in movies in the olden days. There will be a big old comfy chair, a fire crackling, its warmth spreading through the room, and a cat who will sit on your lap and play pad up and down paws on you. There will be hot chocolate, candles burning and no clocks. No pressure to do anything other than read."

"We need magazines in this library too."

"For sure. Glossy mags. I love passing my hand over the sheer glossiness, like glass. Glossy magazine paper has a different smell than book paper."

"We're crazy!" Luke said.

On Friday Luke rushed home from school to change so he could return to The Book Vine.

Braydon was sitting in the lounge, screwed up papers strewn around him.

"What's up?" Luke asked.

"We've got a book assignment due next week and I'm not sure where to start," Braydon replied. A worried crease zig-zagged across his forehead. "Could you help me?"

"Haven't got the time right now, little bro. Maybe later," Luke said, stuffing a banana in his back pack and bounding out the door.

Luke strolled into The Book Vine. His breath halted. Jamie was leaning up against a wooden ladder that was used to access hard-to-reach books on the higher shelves. Her head poked out between the rungs. She was deeply engrossed in an old book she held in one hand. Her long black hair hung down over one side and her pink lip gloss glistened in the light. He swayed as yellow sparks tingled before his eyes. This had to be love.

Jamie came out of her book-world and looked up.

Luke flashed her a smile.

"Hey, I didn't hear you come in." Jamie put the book down.

"You were miles away."

"I wasn't sure whether you'd be here today. I thought you'd have had enough of study being Friday."

"Well, maybe we could finish Chapter 10 and then I'm more than over half-way with the assignment. Hey, what's this?" Luke asked, fingering the lid on an opened box.

"A new shipment of journals. There's some demo products. Do you want to look?"

"Mmm."

Jamie opened the box fully and resting on top, begging to be picked up was an A5 forest green leather journal. Luke carefully took off the cellophane.

Leather straps criss-crossed their way up and down the spine. At the top, the excess strapping dangled over the front of the journal so this could be used as a bookmark. An old compass was engraved into the front cover of the journal.

"Wow," Luke said, running his hand across the smooth top, thinking of his old tatty journal that would soon need replacing. He brought the book up to his nose. "Smell that leather."

He opened the journal to the first blank page. Oh, the poems and stories he could fill its pages. "How much?"

"We'll retail them for about $30," Jamie replied.

"I know Ryan won't give me the money." Luke sighed.

"You really like it, huh?"

Luke nodded. "Never mind. I could get a job but that's out of the question really. How would I fit that in with all the assignments coming out of my ears?"

"Maybe Santa will bring you one." Jamie winked at him. "Actually there's something on the web which you might be interested in. Ever heard of flash fiction?"

Luke shook his head as he and Jamie sat down on the couch.

"It's a short form of highly-focused storytelling of no more than 1,000 words. "There's a competition in one of the city newspapers and I think you should enter."

"I don't know." Luke gulped. His mind swam with doubt. A competition. Putting his work out there for others to critique, judge. *Whack, whack, whack.* The metal ruler reverberated in the back room files of his brain. "Just because I got an A+ in one essay doesn't mean much."

"Don't put yourself down. You've got some real talent," Jamie said, echoing Mr Bligh's earlier words. "Did I tell you I was the editor of our secondary school newsletter and have entered some of these competitions myself? You'd be right up there with all the others."

Luke turned the idea over in his head. Could he really write something worth submitting for a competition? Jamie thought he could. He hesitated, rubbing his chin. It would be hard. He dreaded how long time it would take to get the words written.

Jamie must have seen the doubt lingering in Luke's eyes. "I'll give you a hand," she offered, providing encouragement.

"I appreciate all the help you've given me. I might give this a go." Should he tell her about the journalism scholarship? He was pretty sure she wouldn't laugh at him.

Jamie put her hand gently on his arm sending a bolt of electricity through it. "We can start Monday."

She gazed into his eyes, mesmerising him.

Fuzziness thickened in his head and his heart thudded. A faint summery scent of coconut lotion glimmered around him. He leant in towards her – it seemed the most natural thing in the world to do.

Jamie's hand whispered across his arm.

Luke moved closer. Her breath tapped on his face. Their eyes locked together, neither of them willing to break away.

Luke's lips oh-so-lightly brushed Jamie's soft raspberry-tasting lips. She let out a small sigh. She kissed him back more firmly.

And that was all the certainty he needed, and he continued to kiss her. He floated into her body, floated out of his body, above his body. It was surreal. He melted; the lingering kiss sensual and dream-like, coming from another world.

After an eternity, Jamie slowly pulled away.

Luke's heart rate slowed. His first kiss, and he would never forget it. But in crept the uncertainty, like a chilly fog. What if he hadn't done it right? What if Jamie hadn't liked it?

He stole a look in her direction. Her head rested back against the couch, eyes closed; her face still and serene. She slowly opened her eyes, and her hand fell into his.

Luke rested his head on her shoulder.

They sat in blissful silence. After all the talking, exchanging and debating over the week, words were no longer needed to describe how they felt about each other.

# Chapter 7

Luke spent the week walking as if he was on air. Jamie consumed his every waking thought. He smiled, thinking of Jamie and that kiss. Each moment away from her was endless.

He would rush to The Book Vine after school and together they worked on *The Summer Now Ending*.

Jamie helped him pick a subject for the flash fiction competition and it didn't take long to pull it together. The winner of each of the categories received a small monetary prize plus publication in the young adult writers' magazine, *Fiction Forever*.

Luke dictated his ideas to Jamie. That way he didn't need to write in front of her. Jamie typed everything down, and his confidence grew.

The week progressed. Their work, after The Book Vine closed each day, continued on interrupted by make-out sessions.

"This isn't helping your writing," Jamie said, pushing Luke gently away after a prolonged kissing session.

Luke didn't much care. He was making progress both ways. But an unsettling concern nagged at him. He was falling way behind in his other subjects. And hadn't Ryan mentioned something about upcoming parent-teacher interviews?

"Friday is take-out night," Luke said. "Why don't you come back home with me?"

Jamie said yes and within five minutes they were alighting outside Luke's house, Jamie parking the jeep next to a number of other cars.

"Marcus normally has his mates over on Friday night," Luke explained, as he and Jamie entered the kitchen to raucous laughter, noisy conversation and loud music. "Ryan eats with us too. I don't know where Braydon is." Luke glanced around. No Ryan, no Braydon, no Quinn. What happened to the meal times they used to share together? A sense of disconnectedness trickled through him.

Marcus plus five of his mates munched on pizza, chips, garlic bread and guzzled various drinks.

"Hey brother," Marcus yelled out, getting up from a chair. His brown hair lay in wisps across his forehead, still damp from his shower. "Come and grab some grub; there's a truck load here." He threw Luke a beer can.

"You've brought your girlfriend." Marcus flashed a sly grin at Jamie.

Luke didn't defend the label.

"Jamie? That's right?" Marcus queried.

"Yeah," Jamie replied, eyeing Marcus with caution.

"Would you like a drink?" Marcus asked.

"Sure. Lemonade would be fine."

"There's beer. I'm sure we've got wine somewhere," Marcus said.

"No. No. Lemonade is fine."

"Actually, Marcus, grab me a lemonade as well," Luke said, putting down the unopened can. Luke had tried beer a couple of times but the combination of yeast and other smells made him queasy. Ryan didn't mind him and Quinn drinking but only at the house and with either himself or Marcus present. He was under no illusion of what would happen if Ryan caught him breaking these rules.

Marcus extracted two lemonades from the fridge.

Luke wandered into the lounge to say gidday to Marcus's mates. There was half of one of the large pizzas in a box. This would be enough for him and Jamie. He picked up the pizza box and some other nibbles and turned around. Did Marcus just brush up close to Jamie?

Jamie swerved to the left spilling her drink.

"Hey, what's going on?" Luke asked.

"Just an accident." Marcus raised his palms in the air.

Luke glared at Marcus as he left the kitchen.

"You OK?" Luke stepped closer to Jamie.

"Yeah, fine. Marcus is right. We were kind of trying to be in the same place at the same time and it didn't work." She bit her lip and wound a strand of hair around her finger.

After mopping up the spilt lemonade, Luke suggested they take the food up to his room. "It will be more private."

He took Jamie by the hand, walked her up to the bedroom and closed the door.

They watched *The Matrix* and ate their pizza.

"What is it about this movie you enjoy?" Jamie asked, getting up to stretch her legs when it had finished.

"I don't know." Luke shrugged his shoulders. "Maybe the connection between mythology and religion. Or maybe just an opportunity to escape into virtual reality – nothing is real."

Luke moved over to the window where Jamie stood looking out over the veggie garden. Fruit trees lined the boundary fence. There was a half-worked on car, and a goat grazing beside a triangular hutch.

"You have a goat?" Jamie exclaimed.

"Her name is Minky."

Marcus and his mates had moved outside and were kicking around a ball. Marcus looked up at Jamie and Luke peering out of the bedroom window. Marcus smiled and waved.

Jamie ignored him and moved away from the window.

This could be a good time to get Jamie's opinion on the scholarship. He showed her the advertisement. "Maybe it's out of my league." Luke rubbed his hand down the leg of his shorts.

"I think you should go for it. Writing is obviously your passion and you are good at it."

"I've been thinking about this over the last week. Everything in my life revolves around writing and reading. I've researched journalism as a career." He grabbed Jamie's hand in excitement. "I really want to do this. I just feel apprehensive about doing it by myself. I've only been able to get this far because of you."

Jamie looked down. "Luke, I'm flattered. I really am but it's your drive and desire that has made this possible. It's your vision. I'm just glad I've been able to help channel it more clearly for you."

"There is a small problem though." Luke's face tightened. "Ryan has to sign the application form."

"We'll work on it together. Don't worry; we'll find a way."

Luke squared his shoulders back. Jamie was like his rock. With her he could achieve anything.

The fading light illuminated Jamie's relaxed face. Luke stroked her long, glossy hair as it splayed between his hands. He kissed her lightly on her forehead inhaling her coconut scent. He planted a little kiss on the tip of her nose and then his mouth glided over the top of hers. Every time he kissed her it was like falling into a cloud. He'd the sensation he would keep falling forever.

The door flung open.

Ryan's sturdy build filled the doorway. He stood staring at Luke and Jamie. Luke dropped Jamie's hands and pulled apart from her like a child caught in the middle of doing something naughty.

Jamie stepped back. Her eyes narrowed. She touched her face where Luke's lips were a moment ago.

"What's this?" Ryan's face had frozen like concrete.

"Couldn't you have knocked?" Luke demanded.

"I didn't think anyone was in here. I know where Quinn is but now-a-days you show up at home when you feel like it," Ryan said, the accusation clear. "You shouldn't be having girls in the bedroom."

"Girls. I don't have girls in the bedroom. It's Jamie. Remember?"

"Yes. I remember Jamie," Ryan said, keeping his eyes on Luke.

"And I don't need supervising. I'm not a five-year-old," Luke added.

"Well, you've got no use for a girlfriend at the moment. You need to be concentrating on school. Did you know parent-teacher interviews were held on Wednesday?"

So it had been this week. Why so early in the school year? Why hadn't Ryan mentioned it?

"I thought they were coming up," Luke mumbled.

Jamie had pulled back into the falling shadows.

"Well, the report wasn't great. Your progress in most of your subjects is below average and if you don't pull finger you *will* fail this year." Ryan's hands moved onto his hips. "Does that not mean anything to you? You will leave school with no qualifications and you'll end up on an unemployment benefit. Is that what you want?"

"No, of course not," Luke shouted back. Man, he hated this aggro but Ryan insisted on pushing his buttons. "Did Mr Bligh mention my work?" Luke clung to the chance that all was not as bad as Ryan made out.

"Oh, he said you'd done well in an essay or something," Ryan said, dismissing the comment.

There was Ryan again. Why couldn't he acknowledge that he was doing well in at least one subject?

"You're grounded," Ryan blurted out.

"Whaaat?" Luke's voice rose a pitch higher. None of the brothers had ever been grounded.

"No more girls, Jamie, whatever, until you pull your marks up. You'll be home straight after school and I want an update each day on homework completed."

"What do you really care? You'd never be home to hear it."

"Don't get lippy with me, Luke. Marcus is here most nights – you can fill him in."

Luke rolled his eyes. This was too much.

"I'd better be going," Jamie said. "I'll text you." She threw a feeble smile at Luke as she hurried from the room.

"Did you really have to let rip in front of Jamie? That was embarrassing," Luke yelled.

"I'm not debating this with you." Ryan looked around the room. "Quinn needs to tidy up in here," he added, storming out of the room.

Luke tensed his jaw. How could emotions change oh-so-quickly? He kicked the door shut. Laughter floated up from outside as the guys continued to play ball, carefree.

He spied the print-out with the journalism scholarship details on it. He snatched up the paper. He would never be able to convince Ryan to sign the application papers.

Luke tore up the form trickling the paper into the rubbish bin, his dreams literally ripped apart.

He was back to square one.

# Chapter 8

"I heard that there was a bit of a bust up last night," Quinn said, sitting down beside Luke on the steps outside the house.

Luke glanced sideways at Quinn. "Yeah. How do you know?"

"Marcus told me."

Luke sipped a half-full mug of coffee. The clothes on the line flapped lazily in the breeze, soaking up the mid-morning heat.

"I can't seem to do anything right for Ryan," Luke said, swatting at a passing fly. "He seems to have it in for me."

"Maybe if you just lay low for a couple of days and keep out of his way, give him some time to cool off. I can help you with your homework this week if that would help. We could start tomorrow."

"Won't you be busy with your science projects?"

"Hey, never too busy to give my brother a hand. Don't think that I don't feel the pressure too being the brains of the family. If it makes you feel better, I got a grilling this morning over the mess in the bedroom. He's like a bear with a sore tooth."

"How about I tidy up for you in exchange for some tutoring?" Luke suggested. "It might help keep the warlord off our backs."

"Agreed. Keep your chin up." Trixibelle wandered over to the guys and Quinn stroked her tail. "Sounds like this thing with Jamie is getting intense, huh?"

Luke picked up a stick and scratched a random pattern in the dirt, tracing and retracing the ruts. He wasn't ready yet to talk about Jamie with anyone, including Quinn. Quinn's number one pastime was science stuff. He'd joked that he was more than happy for Luke to be the first to experience the highs and lows in the love department.

"It's like she's my soul mate. No offence to you buddy," Luke quickly added.

The morning song of a bellbird interrupted their conversation.

"If I was choosing some babe to hang out with Jamie would be right up there. She's real cute."

"Well, the family dramas have probably scared her off by now. I've heard nothing from her since last night." Luke checked his cell phone again. No new texts had come in.

"She might be waiting for things to settle down too."

Later that afternoon Luke struggled through his algebra homework. When he could no longer concentrate on meaningless figures and his hand kept writing down words to another poem, he received a text from Jamie.

Relief steadied him.

*Jamie: How are you?*

*Luke: Miss you.*

*Jamie: Me too.*

*Luke: Sorry about last nite.*

*Jamie: Don't worry.*

*Luke: Not sure when I'll be able to see you again.*

*Jamie: At least we can txt.*

*Luke: Not the same.* ☹

*Jamie: I know :**

*Luke: :**

Things were back on track.

The next day Quinn helped Luke catch up with his homework and assignments in which he'd fallen behind. And, as promised, Luke tidied up Quinn's mess.

"I draw the line at making your bed," Luke said.

"Yeah, that's probably a bit slave-ish."

Quinn left to join his mates for a study session. The guy never seemed to want to stop learning.

Luke stood back surveying the bedroom. Both sides now belonged together. He'd one last job to do. He tipped the rubbish tin upside down into a plastic bag. The ripped up jigsaw pieces of the scholarship application form tumbled onto the floor.

He snatched up the paper fragments. What gave Ryan the right to dictate what he could and couldn't do? Why should he let a good chance of getting a journalism scholarship pass him by?

He found the website again with the scholarship details. He printed off another copy of the form. Luke stared at it more resolute than ever that this was his future. Ryan would never sign the form but to hell with him.

He carefully chose what he thought was a sample of his best writing that needed to accompany the application.

Maybe… The seeds of an idea formed but would he be able to follow it through? He shook his head. It wouldn't be right. Scenes pinged around in his mind – the various times he and Ryan had argued and the various discussions they had had over the last six months.  He bit down on his lip, determined.

No movement came from inside the house. Quiet. Luke crept downstairs to Ryan's bedroom.

The double bed was stripped bare. Hair gel, moisturiser, lip gloss and body spray lined one side of the top of drawers. They belonged to Cherie, Ryan's girlfriend. She often stayed over at weekends. She was friendly enough but Luke didn't really know her. Come to think of it he hadn't seen her much lately.

Supervisory, business and viticulture certificates hung proudly on the wall.

Ryan's lap top and a pile of bills sat on the desk in the corner of the bedroom. Luke flicked through the papers and rummaged around. He needed something that had Ryan's signature on it.

Luke sat down at the desk, located a piece of paper and copied Ryan's signature. After a couple of attempts at getting the swirls, whirls and whorls right he copied Ryan's signature onto the scholarship form.

*\*\**

Luke stood at the post box on the side of the road. Little black specks appeared in front of his eyes in the scorching heat. He placed the envelope containing the signed scholarship form on the lip of the post box. He took a deep breath. The envelope teetered back and forward balancing between past and future. It could go either way. Luke gave the envelope a quick push ending the rocking indecision that could now decide his fate. He smiled, a slow smug smile. He'd one-upped Ryan.

The vision of being a journalist – interviewing people, researching, writing the story and seeing his work in print - grew stronger. One day he'd fulfil his dream of working for the BBC or CNN. Better yet, an article in Nat Geo reporting on how the latest tornado season had panned out.

The dream inched that little bit closer...

# Chapter 9

Mid-morning class was algebra, the only class Luke shared with Quinn. Algebra may as well be a completely different language for all he understood of it. Quinn had tried to explain some of the fundamentals to Luke but he just didn't get it.

His thoughts wandered. He'd love to be without the shackles of school, not wasting his time on a subject he'd never use.

The words to another poem he'd been working on were fighting to be heard over the droning voice of the teacher, Mrs White.

*The heart bled*

*The eyes cried*

*The words whispered*

*As they struggled*

*To be part of the world-*

"Luke?" asked Mrs White. "Luke?" The voice came again, calling him back to the present. "Please try and focus on the question."

A rising heat burned in his cheeks as his classmates tittered and sniggered behind him. *Whack, whack, whack. The ruler belted down on his hands.*

"Any thoughts on the answer?" Mrs White asked again.

Luke stared at the Argand diagram. The question related to the formula of $k = i - x$. "Where would k be on the diagram?"

Sweat seeped from Luke's forehead and the suffocating heat of the classroom swamped him. The figures spun on the page. He swallowed hard, his mind a total blank. He'd no idea of the answer. The tops of his hands burned.

"Come on Luke," Zack snickered behind him. "A five-year-old would know the answer to this."

"Yeah," Andrew said, poking a pencil in his back. "You're holding up class."

Quinn leant over and whispered the answer.

The roaring in Luke's ears increased. Too much pressure, inside, outside. He looked blankly at Mrs White.

"I... I..." he stammered, his throat thick, his head light.

More jeering and jibing.

It all became too much. Was he going to faint? Luke rushed out of his chair knocking his pen and pencils to the floor. He had to get out of here. Why was everyone ganging up on him?

The jeering and cheering had reached crescendo.

"Quieten down!" yelled Mrs White.

Luke had had enough. He grabbed his backpack and bolted out of the classroom slamming the door shut.

Luke ran out of the school grounds.

"Hey, Luke. Wait up."

Luke glanced over his shoulder. Quinn was standing at the school gates.

He ran faster towards home, jammed his keys in the front door and threw his backpack on the floor. He doubled over as his breath caught in his lungs. His chest hurt. How would he ever be able to show his face back at class? The humiliation had been beyond belief.

His breathing steadied. He clutched at the pain in his stomach.

All he could think about was Jamie and he needed her – now.

He spied the keys to the ute on the breakfast bar. He collected a couple of beach towels, some cans of drink, two bananas and chips and threw them into a sports bag. He changed out of his uniform, pulling on a T-shirt and board shorts.

Luke climbed into the ute, banged the door shut and shoved the keys into the ignition.

He drove down Resolution Bay Road and parked at the back of Jamie's flat.

His footsteps echoed in the empty shop. Jamie stood at the front counter sorting out a pile of books.

"Luke?" she said, startled to see him. "What are you doing here? Shouldn't you be at school?"

"I was at school."

"What's wrong? You seem agitated."

Luke fidgeted. "It's not working out for me today."

"What do you mean?"

There was a moment's silence. "Have you been to Haven River?" Luke blurted.

"No." Jamie frowned.

"Let's go there now."

"Now?"

"Yes."

"Luke, I can't just leave the shop."

More silence.

"Please," Luke's eyes pleaded. "I want to show you something."

"Can't it wait until I've finished work?"

"No." Luke paced back and forth.

"I don't think it's a good idea. What about Ryan?" she asked cautiously.

Luke scraped a hand through his hair. The mere mention of Ryan's name ratcheted his anxiety up a notch. "Please. We won't be long," he begged.

"OK. OK." Jamie said. She walked over to the front doors and slapped a 'Back in 10 minutes' sign up and locked the doors.

"The ute's parked out back."

Before long they were out on the open road, leaving behind the town. Movement symbolised freedom and Luke's anxiety subsided.

Hot wind swirled inside the car and the tinder dry, golden straw grass whizzed by.

Silence whipped away uneasiness.

Eventually Luke pulled off the highway, over the railway crossing and onto a gravel road, ignoring the 'Private Road' sign. The road ran parallel to a river.

The road grew bumpier and narrower. The long fingers of the willow trees flicked against the side of the ute almost engulfing it, swallowing it, and muffling the traffic noise from the highway.

Luke parked the ute where a gap in the trees gave way to the strong filters of the sun.

"Let's take a look," Luke said. He jumped out of the ute with the sports bag.

Luke walked towards a huge swimming hole, Jamie following behind. Leaves spun and twisted lazily on top of the green-blue surface.

Luke drew in a long breath inhaling the wet and cool, mossy air. The water whispered. In the distance cicadas beat their wings together in a conducted frenzy.

"Wow," she said.

"This is a secret," Luke replied. "We've come here for years. The owners of the road were friends of my folks and we spent many happy weekends here. We'd barbecue, swim and play games down at the river." Luke nodded in that direction. His voice had dropped so low it was almost a whisper, as if he spoke too loud the memories would crash and splinter and be lost forever in the river. "And then we'd come up here and swim in the hole."

He peered into the distance following the twists and turns of the shallow river. It knew where it was going, never having to question its destination. The green banks held the river inside, restraining it from straying on a different path. Were the banks moving closer towards each other preventing the true course of the river, keeping it on the straight and narrow?

"Let's swim," Luke said.

"I didn't exactly bring my swimwear," Jamie said, her brow creasing.

"Not to worry. I have come prepared." He dug around inside the bag, bringing out the towels, sunscreen, food and drink.

"So you kind of planned this?"

"In, like, a minute."

"Did you pack a bikini for me?" she teased.

"Ah, no. Didn't have access to one of those." He grinned cheekily.

Luke pulled his T-shirt over his head and flicked his jandals off his feet. Without hesitating he dived in, creating little splash. He let out a whoop. The coolness washed over him, calming him, washing away his turmoil.

Jamie laughed as Luke continued to plunge and tumble in the water, showing off his best water rat moves.

He came up for air and shook his head spraying prisms of water everywhere.

"Come in," Luke said.

"I can't. I don't have anything to wear."

Luke paused and then said, "Swim in your underwear."

"No. No."

"Come on. There's no one to see you."

"You'll see me."

"I won't look. Much."

"It looks cold."

"It's not too bad. Try it with your feet first."

Jamie pulled off her shoes and stepped gingerly into the water. "Oh God, it's cold!"

"It's warmer under than on top. Come on," he encouraged.

Luke sank down into the water until only his head and shoulders peeked out above the surface.

"I'll face the other way." Luke dog-paddled as he turned his back on Jamie.

"Don't you look," Jamie said, making squealing noises as the cold water enveloped her bit by bit.

Jamie reached out to Luke and plunged his head under water.

He grabbed her arm pulling her down. They both emerged, coughing and spluttering. He had hold of her around the waist and his hands slid over a navel piercing.

Jamie tried to push Luke down but he deftly swerved out of her grasp. He disappeared and came up behind her. Luke's strong arms wrapped around her, caressing her spine, as they disappeared under again. They played, teasing and splashing each other.

"Are you hungry? I've brought some food."

Jamie nodded.

Luke swam over to the end of the hole, leaving Jamie paddling after him. He sat in the back of the ute towelling himself dry. He laid back on his towel and leant his head on his hand letting the sun draw the moisture out of his skin.

Jamie dived a couple of more times frolicking like a mermaid. She emerged from the depths. Her long brown legs, shimmering in the sun, reached for the skies. She squeezed the extra water from her hair, the moisture making it glossier. She was beautiful.

Jamie walked up the slight rise towards the ute, legs and hips sashaying, hypnotising Luke. His eyes riveted to her white underwear, wet and see-through. The right thing would be to look away but he held his gaze, completely paralysed.

"That was so refreshing," Jamie exclaimed, breaking into Luke's daze. She climbed into the back of the ute and wiped herself vigorously with the towel. "I don't know what I'm going to change into," she said, looking around her.

"Everything will dry soon enough," Luke reassured her, willing himself not to look at her.

Jamie settled herself beside Luke. "Are you ready to tell me what's going on?"

Luke brought his fingers up to her lips silencing her. Now was not the time to spill. He was content just to be lost in this world for now.

As if one body, they leant back together. Luke nuzzled his nose into the crook of Jamie's neck, planting little kisses on her until his mouth locked with hers. The strange combination of his warm mouth on her cold lips sent shockwaves through him.

Jamie stretched one of her hands up above her head and Luke reached out to entwine his hand with hers.

He moved closer until his whole body touched Jamie's. His skin against her's, warm from the heat of the sun. The gentle swell of her breasts pressed against his chest. Runaway wet tendrils of hair moulded her face. His breathing shallowed and their chests rose as one.

Heat coursed through Luke's body. This was the point of no return. Luke stopped kissing Jamie and pulled away, hesitating.

"Luke, you're trembling," Jamie whispered.

He couldn't speak but a deep understanding reflected back in her eyes.

"It's OK." She drew him closer to her encouraging him to go on.

He understood now that she'd done this before.

"Don't think. Just do what you feel is right," she encouraged. Her eyes pulled him inside.

Now there was no turning back.

***

On the drive back a calmness, completeness, drifted over Luke, tension released.

He pulled up outside Jamie's flat.

"Would you like to come in?" she asked.

Luke nodded. In his dream-state he was only half-aware of what was happening around him. School was out. Prying eyes from across the street watched Luke and Jamie enter the flat.

Inside they made some sandwiches chuckling over how hungry they were.

He stood next to Jamie their growing closeness emphasised, not just physically but emotionally. This was someone who he could trust completely.

When they had finished eating, Luke held Jamie's hand and his frustrations came tumbling out.

"I don't know what's wrong with me. For as long as I can remember, when I read and write the numbers and words swirl around on the page and I get dizzy.

"I'm hopeless at maths. I can't even remember which my left is and which my right is. Everyone in my class teases me – I'm sure they think I'm dumb. When I write, letters and words get muddled and front-to-back or back-to-front, or whatever it is, which is why it takes me so long to complete my assignments. I can't sleep properly. I'm forever in a perpetual daydream. I'm late for everything. I don't know what's wrong with me." His frustrations tumbled out. "I feel so lost."

"First of all, you're not dumb. You're anything but," Jamie said, tracing a finger along his arm. "Have you seen a doctor?"

"No. I mean, what would I say? What would they say? I'm not sick."

Jamie pondered this for a minute. "What about talking to your teacher or counsellor?"

"I'm not sure. All I know is that I'm only able to make any kind of progress when you help me."

"Maybe this is just some kind of growth spurt."

"I don't think so." Luke ran his fingers through his hair. "I wish there was an answer though." He dropped his head. "You know, I wouldn't have been able to tell anyone else this. You're the only one who'd listen."

"I'm glad you feel you can talk to me. And I'll help you anyway I can." Jamie brushed a hand across his forehead.

He kissed her with tenderness. "Thanks for being there." Luke walked with Jamie to the front door. "I'm not sure when I will be able to see you again."

"We'll play it by ear." She waved as he backed the ute out of the driveway and headed home.

***

Luke pulled the ute up outside the house.

Quinn hurried down the porch steps.

"Are you all right? I've been looking for you everywhere. Why haven't you checked your texts?"

"I'm fine," Luke said, as they made their way into the kitchen.

"Where have you been?"

"I took Jamie to Haven River."

"Oh." Quinn eyed Luke as though there was something different about him but not sure what.

"We went swimming."

"And?"

"Well, you know, we, umm…" Luke started and diverted his eyes.

"Ohhh," Quinn replied.

Luke grinned like a Cheshire cat.

Quinn laughed. "Well, there you go." He reflected for a moment. "Was it good? Or do I really want to know? No, don't answer that. It's not as though I can compare notes," Quinn babbled, his face getting redder and redder.

Luke just kept grinning. He'd shared more than he'd intended to but that was it. He wanted to savour the memory of him and Jamie, close to him for now because without a doubt he was 100 per cent loved up.

*** 

Luke twisted and turned in his bed. Repeated erotic images of him making love to Jamie played over and over in his mind leaving him squirming.

He glanced over at Quinn's empty bed. He must be watching TV downstairs.

Luke's parched throat begged for water. He threw the sheet aside and crept downstairs.

Flashes of light came from the TV. Ryan and Quinn were chatting.

He paused outside the lounge. Someone yawned.

"Hadn't you better hit the sack, bud?" Ryan said.

"Yeah, I suppose," Quinn said. "You know, you might want to cut Luke some slack. He's going through some stuff at the mo and he's finding things a bit tough."

Luke stiffened.

"How far has this thing gone with Luke and Jamie?"

Quinn blew out his cheeks.

Luke pushed his ear closer towards the door. What would Quinn say? Would he dob him in?

"I'm not sure," Quinn said.

Luke bit his lip, glad that the darkness hid the secret in Quinn's eyes.

"I thought he might've said something to you."

"You'd better ask him," Quinn replied, making a quick exit from the room. He almost collided with Luke but he stopped just in time. Quinn stared at him realising that Luke had overheard the conversation.

Luke didn't need to say anything. Quinn had saved his butt.

The bond of brotherhood ran strong.

# Chapter 10

Luke wandered down to the kitchen on Wednesday morning sure that Ryan would already be at work. He avoided Ryan like the plague but at some point they inevitably ended up in the same room together. A cautious truce had developed between them over the last few days. Polite, but hackles raised.

Ryan was sitting at the table eating his breakfast, a stony expression on his face. Luke tipped the cereal into his bowl and sat down at the opposite end of the table.

"I thought you'd be at work by now. Aren't you harvesting?" Luke asked.

"Everything's ticking over smoothly. It's home I'm not sure about," Ryan said, putting down his knife.

Luke gritted his teeth as he flicked through a brochure. Had word got back to Ryan about what had happened in class on Monday and his ditching of school for the rest of the day? Luke knew Quinn wouldn't say anything.

"Is Jamie helping you with your English assignments?" Ryan asked.

"Yes." Luke stuck to a one word answer suspicious of where this was going.

"Is it helping?"

"Yes." He twirled dry cornflakes around in his mouth. A bird bounced on the fence. Time stood still.

"That's good. That's good. Would you like to invite Jamie to dinner on Sunday night?"

What? Luke mentally ticked off ulterior motives. "I'll ask her."

If Ryan was in a reconciliatory mood it might be a good time to mention the brochure. "There was a careers day at school yesterday."

"Oh yeah. How did that go?" Ryan sipped at his coffee.

"Good. I picked up this brochure on journalism as a career."

The air snapped, crackled and popped.

"Luke, we've been over this a thousand times. It's not a good career choice." Ryan got up signalling an end to any further discussion. "And I'm tired of having the same conversation over and over."

Luke didn't want to push it too far in case it jeopardised things with Jamie but he wasn't about to be put off by Ryan's dismissiveness. "Can you just read it? Please Ryan. That's all. Just read it."

Ryan opened his mouth and then shut it again. "OK. OK. But don't think-"

"Just read it. It's all I ask," Luke persisted, handing the brochure to Ryan.

Ryan took the brochure reluctantly turning it over in his hands. "I'm off. Catch you later." He picked up his lunch bag and rushed out the door.

***

Luke swigged at his OJ. If he could just get Ryan to read the brochure it would open the door further. He could be just as persistent as Ryan. He just needed to be patient.

Luke remained at the kitchen table gazing out the window.

"Hey brother, you daydreaming again?" Marcus broke into Luke's thoughts.

"Hey brother."

"You're going to be late," Marcus stated.

The clock on the microwave blinked over to another minute. As usual he'd completely lost track of time.

"Yeah, yeah, yeah," he mumbled.

"There's a party on Friday night at Todd's. Why don't you come? Bring Jamie."

"I don't think that's a good idea. Ryan, you know..." Luke left the sentence hanging.

"Hey, leave that to me."

Luke placed his breakfast dishes in the dishwasher. Having a girlfriend was definitely improving his social life.

He didn't want to be late for school but as he walked down the driveway the rambling bed of dahlias sprinkled with morning dew caught his eye. Vivid burgundy, cerise, light pink and auburn flowers swayed gently in the breeze. He picked a couple of the pink dahlias then chose a few yellow ones, a dark cerise one and plucked a few daisies from a pile growing wild.

He wandered past the school with the flowers in his hands. This would be the first time since Monday he would see Jamie. Would she feel differently about him, and in a good way?

She'd had a head start in the love department. How many had she had? He'd never asked her about her previous boyfriends. He wasn't even sure he wanted to know. Would she compare? Maybe, like Quinn, it was best not knowing. Would she regret what they had done? A million questions tumbled over in his mind. His stomach turned into knots and bubbled. That same feeling when he struggled to read was building up but now for a different reason.

The colourful sandwich board stood outside The Book Vine. Luke spied Jamie through the window as she moved around the shop preparing it for opening. His heart beat faster. He hid the flowers behind his back and entered the shop.

"Hi," he said.

Jamie looked up but Luke's eyes darted off to the side.

"Hi Luke." She smiled. Her eyes said it all. She felt the same way too.

"I brought you these," he said, presenting her with the bouquet.

"Oh! How sweet," she exclaimed. "They're gorgeous."

He returned the smile and his breathing steadied.

Jamie examined the flowers drinking in the beauty of the colour and the perfectly formed petals.

"I think I have a vase somewhere back here." She turned to rummage behind the counter. "Yep. Here it is. How's things going?" she asked, as she arranged the flowers in the vase.

"Well, I don't have algebra today."

"Yay!" She clapped her hands.

"Ryan and I are talking. He wants to know if you'd like to come to dinner on Sunday night."

"Ah, that's good."

"I think he wants to check you out properly. He seems OK about you tutoring me."

"I'd like to come for dinner. It's better to keep Ryan on side than rattle his cage," Jamie admitted.

"Shall we go over *The Summer Now Ending* after school today? There's not much time left."

"Yeah. It would be good to finish it off." She glanced at the clock. "You'd better go."

"Oh and umm… I almost forgot. Marcus has invited us to a party on Friday night."

"Marcus?"

Concern flickered over Jamie's face. Maybe he was pushing things too far. Maybe she didn't want people to know about their relationship yet. Was it because he was still in school? That could be embarrassing for her.

"I'll have a think about it," she replied. Her head tilted to the side.

Luke didn't want to leave without a commitment from her but he gave her a quick kiss on the cheek. He would ask her again later.

# Chapter 11

By Friday Luke had finished not only *The Summer Now Ending* but also the book report.

Working with Jamie had made it easier to discuss the themes in the book. The more he'd read the more he was able to relate to the emotions that grappled Daniel. Luke's emotions strangely mirrored that of Daniel's. He could identify with Daniel's need to make a go of something he didn't really believe in. Daniel seemed to be living in perpetual anxiety, something Luke could relate to.

After some tricky incidents it had all worked out for Daniel in the end. The pull of the country and his love for his girlfriend, Melanie, was too great for him and so he packed in his barely-started life in the city to move back home where his heart truly was.

"It's about knowing what's right for you and following that instinct," Luke said, tapping on the keyboard. He paused for a moment. "I so get that." Would he have the guts to do the same? "It's almost like this book is sending me a message. The timing is spooky."

"I think these set book texts are given to us to read for a purpose. I don't think it's a coincidence. We're reading stuff we can relate to at this time in our lives," said Jamie.

"Maybe I could work that into the report." Luke's fingers and mind coordinated slowly to compile the conclusion. "There. Done."

He was first to hand in his completed assignment on Friday. "I know I'll get a good mark for this," said Luke, as he handed the assignment to Mr Bligh.

Another significant development had occurred during the week.

One never quite knew how the rumours started but as quite often happens they became real. Maybe someone had seen them in the ute, at Café Salt or at The Book Vine. It wouldn't have taken much to put two and two together. But suddenly everyone knew about Luke and Jamie.

As he walked to The Book Vine on Friday after school a car-load of his classmates, including Zack and Andrew, screeched up alongside him.

"Guess who's screwing the new chick in town," yelled out Zack, accompanying it by a rude gesture.

Why did they have to be so obscene?

"Take a hike," Luke yelled back.

When Luke relayed what had happened to Jamie she brushed it off.

"Just ignore them. They're only jealous."

Luke played with the pens in the jar on the counter.

"I'd like to go with you to the party tonight," Jamie said. "Maybe it's better to make a statement about our relationship. We can't sneak around or hide out here forever."

Luke beamed. So she wasn't embarrassed to be seen with him. Their relationship was moving to another level.

Luke and Marcus walked down to the party together that night. Luke had agreed to meet Jamie there and as dusk settled he could just make her out standing on the footpath outside Todd's house.

Luke's eyes skimmed Jamie up and down. She wore tight blue jeans and a cerise top, the colour contrasting against her glossy black hair. The top was cut low enough to expose a hint of her suntanned breasts. Her make-up was darker. As she moved towards him, he caught her summery perfume, a subtle mix of roses and freesias.

They smiled at each other.

"Hi, Jamie," said Marcus, his eyes moving slowly over her body.

"Hi, Marcus," Jamie replied. She grasped Luke's hand firmly.

Music pumped loudly from inside the house. There were a few of Marcus's mates, some other vaguely familiar faces he'd seen around town and some of his classmates. Even Caitlin had turned up.

People mingled outside. Some groups were gathered around the barbecue, smoking, drinking or eating. Others lounged on chairs or stood chatting. A group held out their hands to capture the warmth from the fire burning in a drum. The shape of interlinked couples hinted that they had the advantage of the near darkness.

Marcus passed a beer can to Luke. He seemed to be always shoving alcohol his way. Luke had stopped saying no to Marcus. He either opened the can, took one sip and then left it untouched or it remained unopened.

"You look like a chardonnay type of a girl," Marcus said as he poured Jamie a glass of wine.

Luke dashed into the kitchen, emptied the can of beer down the sink and then filled it up with OJ. Back outside, he struck up a conversation with Caitlin while Jamie introduced herself to some of the girls.

"I'm just popping inside to freshen up," Jamie said.

"Sure thing."

After ten minutes Luke glanced at his watch. Where was Jamie? He went in search for her.

Inside the house he wandered down the hallway. He stopped still in his tracks. Jamie stood with her back against the door, her body tense, hands grasping the doorframe. Marcus's curly brown hair stood out above Jamie's head. She made to move past him but he stayed steadfast, blocking her way. Marcus leaned towards her and reached out his hand. Their heads almost touched and she smiled as he whispered something to her. The body language gave everything away. His brother was making moves on his girl. Black spots appeared in front of his eyes, blurring his vision

"Hey!"

Jamie jumped. Marcus looked sheepish and quickly pulled away.

Luke strode towards the couple. "What are you doing?" Luke glared at Marcus.

"Nothing. I was chatting to Jamie." He crossed his arms. His eyes were on Jamie's chest.

"It looked more than that. Lay off." He lowered his voice. Without waiting for a response, Luke put his hands protectively on Jamie's shoulders and guided her away from Marcus and back outside. Had Marcus deliberately asked them to the party so he could make a move on Jamie?

The freshness of the night air on Luke's face cooled the rising heat in his veins. What would have happened between Jamie and Marcus if he hadn't found them when he did?

"I think it's time to call it a night," Luke said as they walked down the driveway, his voice cold.

"Luke, nothing happened between Marcus and me."

"You guys were standing pretty close together. He was about to touch you. Or had he already touched you?"

"No. Don't read anything more into what you saw," Jamie said, the words tumbling out fast.

"I'll walk you home," Luke muttered.

Jamie grasped his hand but it was stiff and unyielding. "Maybe it wasn't such a good idea to go out together yet..."

"I don't want to talk about it."

They walked back to the flat in silence.

Jamie rummaged around in her bag for her keys.

"I'm sorry," Luke said. "I shouldn't have said those things."

The streetlights threw pale shadows across Jamie's face.

Luke waited for an invite to come inside.

"Do you want to hang out tomorrow?" he asked, squinting at her.

"I really need to catch up with some stuff around the flat. I think it will take most of the day."

"Oh." Was Jamie giving him the brush off? Dread made his breath snag. "So dinner Sunday night still on?" He stood stock still.

"Yes, of course."

Jamie pushed the back door open.

Luke planted a hesitant kiss on Jamie's cheek receiving a lukewarm and unbending response.

Jamie closed the door behind her leaving Luke alone on the door step.

Luke hadn't expected that the evening would've ended so abruptly.

# Chapter 12

Despite Friday night's blip, on Monday after school, Luke rushed past The Book Vine. Something in the window caught his eye. Jamie had displayed the journals in the front window. The forest green one that he'd taken a liking to sat proudly on the stand.

He bounded into the shop and showed Jamie the book report mark – A+.

Jamie was all smiles. Luke rocked back and forth on his feet. His essay mark had not just been a fluke. He'd proved he was a good writer and critical thinker.

"And that's not all," Luke rushed to get the words out. "I won the flash fiction competition. This woman rang me on my cell this morning. I'm going to be published!"

"That's fantastic!" Jamie leant over the counter to give him a kiss. "You've had some small wins but this is significant."

"I can't believe this. This is like confirmation I'm good at something. Like there is a purpose for me. This is the sign my future is in writing."

In between serving customers, Luke and Jamie brought up the Fiction Forever website and pored over the notification of the winners, and there was Luke's name. He bubbled on, his hands moving in buzzy animation. A world of possibilities had opened up for him. He finally had something concrete to prove to Ryan that he not only had the talent but the determination to succeed.

Luke took Jamie's hands in his. "I couldn't have done this without you."

"It was all your hard work and creativity," Jamie said, brushing the compliment aside. But nothing she said could've dampened Luke's joy.

"We need to celebrate," announced Jamie.

At closing time Luke and Jamie scurried around the shop to the back of the flat.

Jamie pulled a bottle of wine out of the fridge.

Luke's mouth fell open. "I can't drink that." He shook his head.

"Why not?"

"I'm in school uniform!"

"Even more reason why. The fact you shouldn't be doing it will make it taste so much better."

"You're a bad influence. You're leading me astray."

Jamie set two glasses on the bench and poured the wine. "Well, just have a few sips then," she teased.

The golden liquid twinkled as it caught the late afternoon sun. Why not? He picked up the glass.

"Cheers, and here's to a great writing career," Jamie said, raising her glass.

They clinked their glasses together and drank.

Luke screwed up his nose at the crispness but after a few more sips his tongue adjusted to the sweet and smooth liquid. It was a definite improvement on beer.

Jamie searched around in her cupboards and produced some cheese and crackers as they continued to discuss, still not believing, Luke's win.

Before long they had both finished despite Luke's resolve that he would drink only a little.

He'd lost all track of time.

"I'd better not tempt fate and miss my 'curfew'," Luke said, standing up. The wine rushed to his head; his feet warm and tingly.

"You'd better take a couple of these," Jamie said handing him some mints.

As he reached over to take the mints, Luke touched Jamie's breast by accident.

"Hey," she said, playfully slapping his hand away.

Nothing could wipe the smile from his face. He settled for a long sultry kiss moistened by wine and mint.

He bounced home, his feet light as air, dizzily and deliriously happy.

Things were looking up.

# Chapter 13

Metal clanged on concrete as Marcus's oil filter wrench fell to the garage floor.

Luke snuck past the garage. He didn't want to have to deal with Marcus who could have any girl he wanted. Just not Jamie. The irony of it. Tiptoeing around Ryan and now avoiding Marcus. Life was getting complicated.

Quinn pulled clothes and pegs off the line, throwing them all into the laundry basket. Trixie marched up to greet Luke, her tail standing straight as a flagpole.

"How does there get to be so much washing?" Luke commented.

"Fact of life, brother. Dirty clothes need washing." Quinn scrunched up his nose. "Have you been drinking?"

"Shh! Not so loud," Luke glanced towards the garage. "No, I haven't. Well, just a little."

"What gives?"

"I was at Jamie's, celebrating. I won a writing competition."

"Way to go!" Quinn slapped Luke on the back.

"I've just won a 100 bucks and I get published."

"Well, there you are." Quinn's smile beamed in pride but quickly faded. "You need to be careful Luke. Getting on the wrong side of Ryan right now won't help. I'm not sure he's all that keen about Jamie. If he found out you've been drinking ..."

"I know." Luke nodded slowly. "I have something real to show Ryan now. He'll come around."

Quinn's face had 'I'm not so sure' written all over it. He tossed the last of the washing in the basket and looked his brother in the eye. "You know, I admire you for having the guts to go after what you want. I know it's not easy for you. But hang on tight to that passion you believe in."

Luke looked away touched at the frankness of Quinn's words. A lump formed in his throat. He just nodded. If he spoke he might tear up. Next to any words that Jamie had spoken, it was the nicest thing anyone had said to him since... when?

But things changed when Ryan came home. He blustered around the kitchen preparing the dinner, Luke trying to stay out of his way.

"When did you get home from school?"

"Just after 3.30," Luke said, avoiding Ryan's eyes but throwing a quick glance at Quinn, who remained poker face.

"Where's Marcus?"

"Still out in the garage," Quinn replied.

"Luke, can you shout out grub's up?"

Luke walked past Ryan.

"Is that alcohol I can smell?"

Luke froze and a hot flush travelled up his face.

"Ah, nah," Luke said. Don't look at Quinn. Don't look at Quinn.

Ryan sniffed the air again.

"I'm sure I can-"

"Must be all those grapes you've been working around all day brother," Quinn said.

"Yeah, must be. Come on Luke. Go and round up Marcus."

Ryan turned back around to the oven.

Luke mouthed to Quinn, "Thanks."

Quinn mouthed back, "Be careful."

Luke ran down the back steps. Whew! Too close for comfort.

# Chapter 14

It was Sunday night.

Luke loitered in the kitchen while Ryan bustled around preparing the dinner.

"I don't know why I suggested a dinner guest tonight," Ryan muttered, stuffing lemon wedges inside the cavity of the chicken. "I've already been at work this arvo. I think I'll need to go back."

Luke shuffled his feet from side to side narrowly missing colliding with Ryan as he opened the fridge. This wasn't going to be good if Ryan was distracted and grumpy.

Ryan poured oil over the vegetables and then bunged the tray along with the chicken into the oven. "Done," said Ryan, letting out a sigh.

The stress and strain of working sixty-hour weeks marked deep creases and frowns across Ryan's jaded face. Ryan looked older to Luke now than ever before.

When Jamie arrived Luke greeted her at the door. He wanted to kiss her – she looked hot, as usual – but wavered when he caught Ryan's eyes. Jamie would make a good impression on Ryan but nevertheless Luke's nerves buzzed like a swarm of bees.

Ryan poured Jamie an OJ and they moved into the lounge. Quinn and Braydon hovered in the background.

Ryan and Jamie chatted. He asked her where she'd gone to school, her work at The Book Vine, what she was going to do next, her hobbies.

Luke leant back on the couch. Things weren't going too bad. In fact, Jamie and Ryan had discovered a common interest in jogging.

"Not so much now," Ryan said. "Work is filling up all my hours but I want to get back into it soon."

"I'd like to do some long distance. Where would be some good places to go?" Jamie queried.

Ryan gave Jamie some options and the two chatted as they swapped running stories.

Luke glanced at Quinn, who winked back, both picking up on the vibe of so far, so good.

Marcus wandered in, gave Jamie a cursory nod and strolled out.

Ryan got up to check on dinner and not long afterwards they were eating. Ryan and Marcus tapped away on their cells. Braydon and Quinn shuffled dishes around and passed them over to Jamie.

The tap, tap, tapping beat out the next poem in his head –

*Texts*

*Disconnect us*

*From you and me*

*And family –*

Braydon's observation about the weather brought him back.

"If you think we are experiencing a heatwave apparently it got to 45 degrees in Sydney on New Year's Day," Braydon commented.

"Well, I hope the good weather continues here. It'll upset the harvest otherwise."

Jamie dished up the raspberry cheesecakes she'd brought for dessert. Everyone stood around in the dining room spooning cheesecake into their mouths chatting.

"I've been doing some research lately around Luke's learning difficulties," said Jamie.

Luke's head snapped straight up and his spoon clattered onto his plate. What? What was she on about?

"Luke has a number of symptoms," Jamie continued, extracting some paper from her bag and reading them out. "Algebra difficult to comprehend, daydreaming, confuses left from right, writing shows repetitions, omissions, transposition ...." She spoke faster and faster, her words falling over one another.

"Whoa! Whoa!" Ryan interrupted, shaking his head in confusion. "What's this all about?"

Jamie continued without skipping a beat. "There are reasons why Luke struggles so much at school. This list explains a whole heap of things."

"I think the reasons are more to do with distractions," Ryan responded belligerently.

Luke's left eyebrow twitched as it sometimes did when he was nervous. What on earth was Jamie doing? Was she deliberately trying to aggravate Ryan? Things had been going so well tonight. He shot her a warning glance.

"You know, the best thing for Luke right now is for him to knuckle down and get good grades." Ryan crashed his plate down.

"I think Luke has dyslexia," Jamie blurted out.

"What?" everyone said in unison.

An icy chill crept over Luke's head and snaked down the rest of his body. All eyes turned towards him. Dyslexia? It sounded like a disease. He'd heard about the condition. But was that what he had? He rocked from side to side, a sense of panic building.

"Luke's strengths – his creativity, his writing – need to be encouraged. He's really gifted. He got an A+ for the book report. Winning the flash fiction competition proved that."

Ryan ignored the reference to the book report grade. "What flash fiction competition? I don't even know what that means," Ryan yelled in frustration. He stood with his hands on his hips.

"You haven't told him?" Jamie asked, her eyes widening.

"No… No…" Luke stuttered. He laced his hands behind his head. "He hasn't been around. I wanted to wait …"

"So that's what you've been spending your time doing?" Ryan shouted. His eyes smouldered. "I warned you. Christ, Luke. What do I have to do to make myself more clear?"

Luke dropped his hands and shrank back towards the wall.

Quinn, Marcus and Braydon stood wide-eyed and spellbound.

Jamie's eyes blazed and her voice raised, matching Ryan's in volume. "You shouldn't yell at him like that. He tries very hard. He tries harder than anyone I know. Dyslexia has been preventing him from achieving his full potential. You need to get him to take some tests. He needs help."

"This is unbelievable. Who do...." Ryan started. He shook his head. "Who do you think you are? Telling me what I should do and what education choices are best for Luke. I would've recognised the signs of dyslexia. Really! A 17-year-old girl who knows it all."

"That's unfair. I was only-," Jamie flashed back.

"It was a mistake asking you over. Stop interfering, and stay away from Luke." Ryan pointed a finger at Jamie.

Luke focused on a dirty spot on the ceiling. His body pressed hard against the wall. If he closed his eyes tight maybe he would disappear into it. He chanced a look at Jamie.

"You'd better go," Ryan finally said. Hostility dripped from his voice.

Jamie stood riveted to the spot.

"Now would be good." Ryan crossed his arms.

Jamie didn't budge. She refused to be silent. "Don't you want to even consider what I've just said?"

Ryan stared her out. "Don't. Challenge. My. Authority."

Jamie's eyes pleaded at Luke. Tears welled up in her eyes.

Luke snapped his head back towards the ceiling. Out of the corner of his eye, Jamie stuffed her notes back into her handbag. She hurried out of the room and banged the front door behind her.

Luke rushed up the stairs, head down and bolted into his room. The second door of the night slammed shut like a gunshot exploding.

*** 

Luke sat on his bed in the dark.

"You want to talk about it?' Quinn asked.

"No. I just want to be left alone."

"I'll leave you be." Quinn placed a reassuring hand on his shoulder as he left the room. "I'll be downstairs if you change your mind."

Luke nodded.

He sat, the darkness enveloping him.

He couldn't believe what had happened.

His heart pounded. He'd shared his confidences with Jamie and she'd betrayed him. He hadn't expected that she would let it all out like that in front of everyone, leaving him vulnerable and exposed. He'd been so certain that she'd understood him. But he'd been wrong. She was no different from the classmates who teased him.

He swallowed the bitter anger. He could no longer sit.

He paced back and forth, restless.

Why had she done this? She'd wrecked everything and the thought of facing Ryan again made him want to throw up.

One thing was certain. He would never forgive her – ever.

# Chapter 15

Luke had waited for Jamie to contact him to apologise. But there had been no phone call, no text, no visit, nothing. She obviously didn't know how much she'd hurt him.

By Friday the anger had disappeared and the aching in his heart returned.

Jamie's surprising revelation and Ryan's persistent tirade, like a broken record, of what he thought Luke should do with his life tore him in two.

He missed Jamie; she'd become so much a part of his life. He'd turned to her when the going had got tough. She said the things he needed to hear, the little words of encouragement. She'd a belief that he could be whatever he wanted to be.

Luke and Ryan's relationship deteriorated further. Whenever Ryan spoke to him, his words belittled, his tone terse, frosty.

Apart from school, Luke was banned from going anywhere. Home was now his prison, driving him slowly crazy.

If something didn't give way soon, he would explode.

# Chapter 16

On Monday all the teachers plotted together to give out screeds of assignments. There was one due for every subject all within a week of each other.

Luke's heart rate plunged up and down all day long. It slowed right down when Mr Bligh, his English teacher, assigned a new book for reading. And then it increased again. This was an assignment he would have to tackle on his own.

Mr Bligh waited until all the students had left and then called Luke over to him.

"Why didn't you tell me you'd won a flash fiction competition?" Mr Bligh asked.

"I kind of forgot." The gloss had dissipated gradually over the week.

Mr Bligh smiled. "Well, well done. You've been making excellent progress lately. Have you given any thought to what you might do at the end of the year?"

"Ryan and I don't exactly agree on the direction my future should take."

Mr Bligh had taught Ryan four years earlier.

"Would you like me to talk to him?" Mr Bligh asked, tilting his head to the side.

"No. No." Luke fobbed him off. "I'm sure something will work out eventually."

Mr Bligh closed his briefcase. "Luke, you're well aware this is a small town and people talk."

"Yeah." Luke's eyes flicked sideways. Where was this going?

"You're seeing the woman who is at The Book Vine?"

"I was seeing Jamie briefly but it's over," Luke said. The words sounded hollow and detached and he swallowed hard over the lump in his throat. What did his relationship with Jamie have to do with anything?

"I'll come straight to the point." Mr Bligh paused a moment and then carried on. "There is some suggestion that the work you submitted for the flash fiction competition was not your own."

"What? What do you mean?"

"Did Jamie write the flash fiction?"

"No, no. She helped me type it and she'd some ideas but it was all my own work."

"Do you realise this is serious? That you have been accused of cheating?"

"I... I... I haven't cheated." Luke gulped. How much of the work had he done had been just his? Had he over-estimated Jamie's input? *Had* he cheated?

"I would never cheat," Luke said. He needed to gain control of the situation.

Mr Bligh stared at Luke for a moment studying him and then said, "I believe you. I don't suspect your integrity but you understand that I needed to ask?"

Luke nodded still unsure as to whether he'd 'cheated'.

"I also need to ask you whether your English assignments are original?"

"Yes, yes, of course." *If I could just stop stammering I wouldn't sound so guilty.*

"Good. Thank you for being honest. I hope you enjoy the new book."

Luke wanted to be far away from school so he could think more. The temperature had cooled over the last week and rain had been predicted. He barely noticed the greying clouds gathering over the hills and the autumn chill as he replayed the conversation in his mind.

It would take a fair bit of analysis to figure out how much of the work had been his compared to Jamie's input. It had never crossed his mind that he'd submitted work that hadn't been wholly created from his own mind, his own hand. If this might've been the outcome he would never have entered the stupid competition in the first place. He didn't need this hassle.

Why didn't he get Jamie's opinion? He perked up for a moment but a wave of blue swallowed him. She'd made no attempt to contact him. Nothing could make it right now.

The gloomy prospect of a new school week coupled with stacks of work to complete and his morality in question, rightly or wrongly, hung over him like a big black cloud.

# Chapter 17

The week dragged.

Luke struggled with the assignment deadlines. He concentrated on English, his favourite subject, but without Jamie's help everything took twice as long.

After school Friday finally arrived but it held little reprieve. Most of the weekend would be consumed with his studying.

The decline in the weather that had threatened all week finally arrived and light rain fell as Luke walked home. The delicate beads of moisture settled on his face dissolving under his skin. It carried with it the sensation that something wasn't quite right. He couldn't put his finger on it or even describe it. His stomach quivered, the intensity increasing by the hour. Maybe it was just the change in the weather.

"It would rain now while we're harvesting," Ryan cursed, staring out the kitchen window as Luke walked in.

Luke grunted. The less he and Ryan engaged in conversation the better.

When Marcus arrived home from work there was a quick discussion regarding takeouts. Pizza got the vote and Marcus dialled in the order.

"Shouldn't we wait for Quinn?" Braydon asked.

"One of his mates is dropping him off. His science class visited the salmon farms and the boat was due back an hour ago," Ryan replied, eyeing the clock on the wall. "He shouldn't be too far away. By the time pizza arrives Quinn should be here too."

The pizza arrived shortly but there was no sign yet of Quinn. The guys dug in half-heartedly saving some food for their brother.

Amongst the eating the familiar scenario played out as Ryan and Marcus tapped on their cells. Braydon concentrated on the TV, something about a cat attacking a dog.

Luke grabbed a couple of slices of pizza. Lunch was a life-time ago. He shivered. That sense of disconnection had widened, threatening the stability of a slow fracturing family. The quivers in this stomach continued to nag at him. Something wasn't right. His eyes diverted to the clock. Shouldn't Quinn be back now?

Ryan's cell rang. "Ryan Conway," he said. He threw an empty box onto the kitchen bench and then stopped in mid-stride. "What?" he said, chilliness creeping into his voice, creeping into the room.

Something was wrong, something terribly wrong. Ryan's face turned white with worried concern.

"Oh God," Ryan replied.

All movement in the kitchen halted. Eyes fixed on Ryan who was shaking his head from side to side.

"We'll be right there," Ryan's voice strained as he rang off.

Luke's stomach jerked.

126

"Guys quick. There's been a bad car accident. Quinn's seriously hurt. We need to get to the hospital."

There was a moment's silence and then everyone spoke at once.

"What?"

"Is he OK?"

"Who were you talking to?"

Disbelief, horror and fear swept over Ryan's face.

Everyone scrambled out the door and crowded into the car, Ryan pulling away before all the doors were shut. He hightailed it down the driveway. The light rain had turned into solid drops making visibility poor.

Luke's bottom lip trembled. He wiped his clammy hands over his jeans. There was only one thing on his mind – please let Quinn be OK.

# Part 2

In the depth of winter I finally learned that there was in me an invincible summer.

Albert Camus

# Chapter 18

Everything blurred for Luke.

Reality distorted.

Long unseen relatives shook his hand and said how sorry they were.

Everyone dressed in black.

Jamie with silent tears rolling down her face.

Flowers.

The senior school attending the funeral.

The school flag at half-mast.

People delivering food to the house.

More flowers.

Ryan, Marcus, Braydon and himself embraced together in a distraught hug.

Someone giving him a pill, telling him it would take the edge off.

Numbness.

Automatically doing what people told him to do.

Jarring lights.

*Why were there so many flowers?*

Someone asking him if he would like to choose the music for the service.

Holding Braydon's hand.

A coffin.

A priest saying something.

People telling him everything would be all right.

Bowed heads.

Girls lighting candles.

Caitlin saying something.

A photo of Quinn.

His face was wet. *Was he crying?*

Too many people. Too much noise.

The lonely bedroom.

*Hell, he missed Quinn.*

Darkness.

Numbness.

Was there no end to the pain?

Nothing mattered.

All he wanted to do was be left alone. Forever.

# Chapter 19

Luke moved through the days on auto-pilot. His brothers' reaction to Quinn's death penetrated dully in his numb-minded state.

Braydon would cuddle Trixie or stroke Minky, seeking some kind of comfort through touch. The animals were always there, unchanged, oblivious. Braydon was more reassured in their presence than in the unsettled world that was suddenly his. The tears were silent, the sobbing not so much as he buried his head in Trixie's fur.

Everything in his soul was telling him to reach out to Braydon but his feet remained rooted to the spot, his arms hanging lifelessly by his side. He turned and walked away.

Ryan was never home, away twelve hours straight, throwing himself into his work, even on Sunday. But why didn't he want to be at home? Maybe it was the memories. Maybe if he kept working he wouldn't have to think about life, living, his brothers and how everything was falling apart.

And Marcus? He'd no idea.

Nobody spoke to one another.

His brothers were lost, slowly drifting further and further apart.

# Chapter 20

Luke stared listlessly into the blackness. Nights were the worst and the bedroom was like a prison cell. He'd run the gauntlet of a hundred negative emotions and in every intensity.

He could not break through the pain and bewilderment. How could Quinn leave him? And in such a horrible way. It had all happened so unexpectedly. No warning, nothing. One day he was there; the next, bam! he was gone. Life was cruel and it was tearing his family apart, piece by piece. First his folks. Now Quinn. Who next? Ryan? Marcus? Braydon? Himself? Until there was no one left? So why care anymore? What was the point?

After the initial shock had worn off it appeared life would keep going, with or without Quinn. But Luke wasn't ready to accept this. If he could continue to wallow in grief forever then that was fine by him. His stomach rumbled. When had he eaten last? Like everything else, food held little interest to him now.

The lonely bedroom. He and Quinn had never slept more than four nights apart. The sleepless nights that had so often consumed Luke before had been partly bearable by Quinn's soft, steady breathing.

He lay awake straining to hear the faint breathing. He was sure he could hear it now.

"Quinn?" he whispered, waiting for a reply.

But there was never a reply.

There would never, ever be a reply.

*** 

Luke was one step removed from himself, like he was experiencing everything through a fog. Nothing anyone said registered in his brain. He'd vague recollections of responding in one syllables.

Dazed, he floated through his first day back at school. Moving through the corridors, students nodded at him. Some touched his arm and said things like, "Hey Luke", "Chin up", "Sorry about what happened." A sombre mood had fallen over the school. Two of Quinn's mates were still in hospital, one in intensive care.

And to add misery upon misery, first class up was algebra.

Luke slipped into the classroom. Conversation stopped and people stared at him. He sat down in his normal seat but the one beside him remained empty. He stared at it, willing for Quinn to appear, to be convinced that this was all a bad dream.

His eyes stung at the threat of tears. His hands shook and he gasped for air as the lingering anxiety made its way to the surface.

Hot, bright lights flashed on and off in his head. He couldn't do this. He swallowed repeatedly. Everything was about to boil over. All he wanted to do was run. He had to get out of the room.

He snatched up his bag, fighting the rising nausea, and darted to the toilets dry retching into the toilet bowl. There was nothing in his stomach to expel. He collapsed against the wall and tiredly wiped beads of sweat from his lip. There would be no Quinn to come and check on him this time.

He was unsure how long he sat on the cold concrete floor but eventually he struggled onto his feet. His limbs shook, unsteady. His mouth tasted like the inside of a rubbish bin. There was no way he was going back to algebra. That was the last algebra class he would ever attend.

*** 

Another sleepless night.

Luke in a brain-fuddled state crept downstairs for a glass of water.

He stopped when he got to the bottom of the stairs. Someone was still in the lounge. His ears strained at the muffling, moaning, sighing of two people. Luke recognised those sounds. The noises were coming from the couch. He edged closer as the moaning increased.

Empty screwed up cans lay on the coffee table, the stench of beer and the cloying sickly-sweet aroma of cheap perfume hung in the air.

He peered over the side of the couch. A woman with her eyes shut, black hair like Jamie's, sprawled over the edge of the couch. Marcus pumping up and down.

Luke gagged. He covered his mouth and backed away. So this was how Marcus was dealing with his pain? He'd heard rumours he was hitting the grog – and the girls – hard.

Silent tears trickled down his face. He trudged up the stairs, not caring whether Marcus heard him.

Luke fell onto his bed and pulled the sheet up over his head burrowing further and further down, like a rabbit escaping from its enemy.

Dawn broke. Built-up tension in Luke's shoulders drained away along with the night and all her demons. But dread cycled back to him. Another empty day had begun.

Luke turned over in bed pulling the covers over his head to shut out the light. The house was still. It was always still now. Did he live on an empty island?

Through one eye the clock blinked 8:00.

He'd be late for school but he didn't care.

He turned his back on the clock and drifted into an uneasy sleep.

***

Bunked and funked.

Luke had bunked school for three days. But he hadn't been missed. No one had rung or texted him. What kind of grilling would he get from Ryan? He dismissed the causal thought. He hadn't seen Ryan for three days.

His gritty eyes bored into the tornado poster. Was it his imagination or did the storm clouds seem blacker, more turbulent, menacing? The blackness encroached over the edges of the poster, seeping over the walls, down towards the floor searching to envelop his body.

He closed his eyes. He'd fallen into a big, black, dark hole and he could see no way out.

*** 

By Friday his limbs were twitching. He was ravenously hungry. And he smelt.

He took a shower, turning up the hot water until it was almost scalding. He vigorously soaped himself. Could he wash away all the sadness too? He stood, immersed in the hot water that rushed over him creating a cocoon.

He got out of the shower and wiped the steam off the mirror. He'd lost weight and dark circles threw shadows under his eyes.

Down in the kitchen the fridge was overloaded with food.

Luke devoured cereal, toast, a glass of milk, OJ and a banana.

Clean and fed he wandered around the house with no purpose but a renewed sense of energy buzzed in his blood.

What to do? What to do?

Luke eyed the ute parked outside. Yep. He needed to get away.

He drove into town, uncaring as to who might see him when he should be at school.

He parked the ute down the other end of town avoiding The Book Vine. He strolled into the town's only tattoo studio. He'd never been inside; there had never been a reason to. But his perceptions of a dark, dingy, musty shop with head-banging tattoo artists merrily scratching away on unmarked skin fast disintegrated.

The modern studio's spotlights emphasised the gleaming wooden floors and framed photos of some amazing tattoos. An old Pink Floyd song played in the background.

"Hey," greeted the male tattoo artist.

"Do you have a tattoo catalogue I can look at?"

"Sure." The guy came out from behind the counter and they sat down on a black chair. Impressive looking skulls, crosses, brambles and volcanoes covered his arms. He pulled some folders out of the drawers. "What were you thinking of?"

"Um, not sure." Luke slowly turned the pages. "I think I'll know it when I see it."

"I'll leave you to browse. If you need any help just holler."

Luke's eyes wandered over the pages. Nothing spoke to him. He liked what Marcus had done – tattoos of his brothers' birthdates. A hazy image beckoned to him. He wanted a tattoo that would honour

Quinn. The tattoo would represent something that couldn't be broken, even in death.

Quinn loved science just as much as Luke's passion for reading and writing. He'd read about the Tree of Life, a spiritual symbol. The Tree of Life represented wisdom, protection, beauty, redemption, abundance, strength and God's grace. He didn't care too much about God's grace, tasting bitterness. If God cared, Quinn would still be alive.

"Do you have any Tree of Life tattoos?" Luke asked.

"Yep." The tattoo guy directed Luke to another catalogue. "These ones here are popular." He pointed to a few photos of big leafy, green trees. Some had huge, ugly, gnarly root systems. In the corner of the catalogue was a photo of a small and neat tree overflowing with leaves. Tiny roots appeared from underneath the base of the tree. The overall feel was vitality in a compact way without being intimidating. He liked it.

"This one would be kind of cool," Luke said.

"Good choice." The guy looked sideways at Luke. "How old are you mate?"

"Sixteen."

"You do realise that parents' permission is required if you are under the age of eighteen."

"No, I didn't." Luke's shoulders sank. Typical.

"I can give you the forms and once they're signed we can go for it."

Luke stood up. "Forget it." Ryan wouldn't give his consent. He'd road blocked everything else he'd tried to do. Why would this be any different?

The tattoo guy shrugged. "Sorry, son."

Luke banged the door shut. Why was it that every time he made a decision about something obstacles slammed into him? His blood verged on boiling point. He kicked a can into the gutter as he strode back to the ute.

The sun disappeared behind a cloud. The greyness bore down on him like a heavy cloak.

His cell went off. It was a text from Marcus.

Marcus: Party at Kelvin's 2nite. R u in?

His stomach flip-flopped. Marcus and the Jamie look-alike from last night.

He stared out down towards the harbour as he watched the ferry berthing.

He needed a change of scenery, some way of blowing off steam.

Luke texted out, Yep, see u thr.

# Chapter 21

Luke had just got home, keys to the ute still in his hand, when a car screeched to a stop outside. Luke glanced out the window. Ryan. What was he doing home? His heart dropped. Ryan had found out he hadn't been at school.

Maybe he could creep out the back but it was too late. He swallowed hard preparing himself for the confrontation that was about to come. Ryan burst through the front door before Luke could make another move.

"Why aren't you at school?" Ryan demanded.

"I don't know. Just not feeling up to it." Luke shrugged.

"You haven't been at school all week. I've just had a call from your teacher so I've had to leave work to come and sort this out. What have you been doing all this time?"

"Just hanging out."

A silence hung between them. Ryan lowered his voice. "I know it's hard. But we've got to move on."

Luke stared at the floor, his mind a complete blank.

"Talk to me," Ryan demanded.

"Talk? That's hard to do when you're yelling at me all the time."

"I'm trying to help you."

"I don't want your help. I don't need anyone's help. I just want to be left alone." Luke pulled his hands up behind his head.

"You need to go back to school."

"I don't want to go back to school."

"No isn't an option. You're going to school on Monday. How are you going to make up the time you've lost?" asked Ryan, his words coming out in a fast explosion.

"I don't know and I don't care."

Ryan spied the keys in Luke's hand. "Give me the keys."

"No!"

"Give me the keys!"

"No!"

Ryan grabbed Luke's arm and with his other hand yanked on the keys. Luke's grip tightened as he pushed back on Ryan's shoulder. Luke hung onto the keys as though his life depended on it. Ryan pulled back, his face set in determination. Luke released his grip as Ryan's strength gradually overpowered him. Another battle Ryan would win. It was no use. The urge to fight fizzled. His hand went limp. He threw the keys on the floor wincing as they clanked on the tiles.

"You know what? Fuck it. I don't need this."

Ryan froze.

"Have the keys. I don't care." Luke flung his hands in the air. "I'll walk – anywhere – just so you're not in my face." He stormed out of the house banging the front door as loud as he could.

The little bit of control he'd desperately clung to over the last week trickled away and along with it his reason for being. He'd lost the meaning of what family meant and he had no idea how to fix it.

# Chapter 22

The loud pumping music throbbed in his head. Cigarette smoke thickened inside the house. Luke coughed and drifted outside seeking cleaner air.

The Jamie look-alike hung off one side of Marcus. A blonde loitered on the other. Marcus had no problem attracting more than one woman. Luke couldn't even keep his.

"Hey brother," Marcus said.

The blonde smiled at Luke.

"Help yourself to the grog." Marcus nodded towards a stash of cans and bottles sitting in an ice-filled chilly bin.

Luke ignored the beer. A bottle of chardonnay beckoned him. Images of chardonnay and a laughing Jamie blurred.

There were no fancy glasses this time so he poured the wine into a plastic cup until it almost overflowed.

He gulped down the first couple of mouthfuls, the intoxicating sweet warmth of the wine hitting his feet almost immediately.

The music continued to bang away at his head. Loud conversations and laughter grated up and down his spine.

He lurked in a dark corner. He swigged some more and drained the cup empty.

The blonde disengaged herself from Marcus and walked towards Luke. She appeared to float towards him.

"You're Marcus's brother, right?"

Luke winced at the loud, brassy voice. "Yeah." Luke wasn't in the mood for conversation. He busied himself by pouring another wine. His unsteady hand slopped the liquid over the side of the cup.

"Wanna pour one for me?" she purred, offering her cup.

Luke concentrated on not spilling the drink.

"You don't say much," the blonde said.

Luke remained silent.

"Maybe you're more about action, like Marcus." She brazenly touched his thigh.

Luke jumped.

"Gee, you're really tense. A shoulder rub then?"

She moved behind him and massaged his shoulders. Luke fought the paradox of wanting to recoil from human contact to giving himself up to her soothing touch. Firm hands manipulated his tense muscles. The wine woozed in his head.

A couple were seriously making out. Erotic pictures of Jamie flashed through his mind.

The blonde's hands swept lower down his back.

Well, if Jamie didn't want him anymore somebody definitely thought he was OK.

Hands slipped over the front of his jeans and expert fingers fawned him. He closed his eyes and shifted, giving himself up.

A warm mouth sucked on his neck. He tilted his head back. His body pulsed with heat.

If this continued it would lead to where he didn't want to go. It would be good for his ego. It flattered him. But it wasn't the blonde who had him so heated. He pushed the blonde away and stood up. He drained the cup again, cracked it and then threw it aside.

"Well, thanks for nothing." The blonde scowled and drifted off looking for her next prey.

Luke swayed to the side. His feet wouldn't move as fast as he liked but a moment of clarity held the answer.

Luke had a score to settle and he wasn't waiting any longer.

***

Luke pounded on Jamie's front door. A light turned on in the hall. The door opened.

"Luke, what on earth?" Jamie said, squinting at him.

"I want to talk to you," Luke slurred as he pushed past her, striding into the room bringing with him a stench of wine and cigarettes. His eyes darted to and fro.

"My God. You're drunk!"

"You had no right to just spill out whatever it is you think is wrong with me. In front of everyone, particularly Ryan. You humiliated and embarrassed me. If you think I have dyslexia you could have at least mentioned something to me first without blabbing it out like that. You know, you can't possibly understand how I feel or what I'm going through. You think you have the answers to everything. Your life all mapped out for you. Well, it's not that simple. I trusted you. I thought you were my friend."

He lurched towards her.

Jamie stepped back.

"Get out," she said, her voice breaking as Luke reached out for her.

She took another step backwards.

"Get out!" she yelled again, pointing towards the door. "You know nothing about me. Who are you to judge?"

He pulled back but stared at her in defiance.

Jamie glared straight back. "Get out!"

Luke held his ground for a moment and then stamped out of the room not even bothering to close the door behind him.

# Chapter 23

Luke had expected an apology from Jamie. For her to understand that she'd let him down but she'd yelled at him too. Just like Ryan.

The walk home wasn't doing anything for his frazzled nerves. The more steps he took the more negative energy flowed through his body.

He raced up the stairs to avoid Ryan.

Luke switched on the bedside table light in his room. No, their room. He couldn't think of it as just his room yet. He'd forbidden anyone from entering. He'd left Quinn's side untouched.

An eerie sound, close to a laugh, rumbled in his mouth. His eyes flicked over the paradox of the two sides of the room; the mess on Quinn's side, his in order.

He needed to tidy like it was some sort of self-cleansing ritual.

Luke hurried around to Quinn's side. He smoothed over the bed, straightened up papers, dumped stuff into the rubbish bin, folded up clothes, and threw things into drawers.

After half an hour he was done. He took a deep breath. Everything now looked as one and belonged together.

But something wasn't right. This wasn't normal. Quinn's side rarely looked like this.

Where are you Quinn? The words reverberated around in his head like an out-of-control pinball.

Waves of despair rolled over him. He wanted life back to how it was before. He would do anything to have Quinn back, the messiness, all of it.

Luke lashed out pushing piles of Quinn's books off onto the floor. Thud! He jumped, his nerves cracking. He pulled out a drawer and emptied stuff onto the desk. He let out a cry as he kicked the rubbish bin hard knocking it over and spilling its contents. He ripped the covers completely off the bed. He turned to the set of drawers and swiped everything off it. Test tubes, more books, empty glasses, pens, pencils, molecule models and a lava lamp all crashed to the floor. Liquid in all colours splashed up the sides of the bed creating a kaleidoscope of colour confusion. His eyes focused on the one remaining item on the desk; a frame which held a photo of him and Quinn celebrating their thirteenth birthday. He picked it up and hurled it at the opposite wall where the glass splintered and tinkered to the floor.

The door flung open.

"What's going on in here?" Ryan yelled, looking around him in astonishment.

Built-up pressure in Luke released like an overflowing dam. He stood in the middle of the room sobbing uncontrollably, tears pouring down his face, his fists clenched.

"Oh, Luke, Luke, Luke." Ryan rushed to Luke and wrapped his arms hard around him. Luke's knees buckled, and they both collapsed to the floor. "Let it out," he said.

"Why? Why?" Luke cried over and over.

Ryan stroked Luke's head like a lioness comforting her cub. He pressed his head against Luke's, clasping him closer. Their bodies trembled and their tears merged.

Luke and Ryan clung to each other and cried their hearts out, united in grief.

* * *

Luke struggled up into a sitting position wincing at the stiffness in his body. He and Ryan had fallen asleep, arm in arm, on the floor. The clock blinked over to 11:30.

Luke rubbed his sleepy eyes, the mess in the room coming in and out of focus. What had happened? Recall drifted slowly back. He glanced at Ryan, who was still asleep, and a wave of compassion gripped him. So Ryan hurt too. He'd seen a vulnerability in Ryan he'd rarely witnessed before. So different from the tough and in-control Ryan.

Luke quietly rose to his feet and arranged Quinn's duvet on top of Ryan. He took a final look at his brother. Would he and Ryan ever understand one another? Instead of experiencing a calm from tension released it had an opposite effect. He was wired and on edge. He needed to keep moving. He wiped his tongue over his lips.

149

Did he dare take the ute out?

Luke's search for the keys proved fruitless until he found the spare set in the pantry, hanging on the hook, beckoning.

Luke started up the ute. The grumble of thunder echoed over the hills and huge drops of rain slapped onto the windscreen.

He switched on the radio. The hypnotic and frenetic *Talk* by Coldplay rang out loud. Yep. The soundtrack to my life. A heavy gloom descended down on him.

He gunned the ute down the drive. A strange mix of warm air cooling by the impending rain filled the air. In the distance the horn of the freight train blared out. The low dense thundering of the wheels reverberated through his soul. He sped on. The train rumbled closer. A mournful whistle filled the night. The wind keened through the ute. What did any of this matter? He'd reached breaking point.

Luke's foot pressed harder on the accelerator. He could beat the train and if he didn't, so what? His eyes blurred with tears. It was much closer now. The sound of metal on metal. The train came into view from behind the trees and he took a sideways glance at the golden light glowing at the front. His foot remained on the accelerator. He'd often watched Marcus and his mates play chicken in their cars with the train. Their whoops echoed around him as they either appeared to stop just in time at the crossing or crossover, a hair's breadth to spare.

The ute lined up to be on an exact collision course with the train.

45 seconds to impact.

35 seconds to impact.

His foot pressed down a touch harder.

30 seconds …

But this was not how this was going to end. Sobbing, he yanked his foot off the accelerator and braked hard. The ute skidded to a stop metres from the crossing, and the train careered past.

Luke sat still in the darkness fright holding him rigid as something Quinn had said came back to him. *"I really admire you for having the guts to go after what you want. Hang on tight to that passion you believe in."*

And that was exactly what he would do. He would find the courage to stand up to Ryan and go after what he wanted. He couldn't imagine a life without writing playing a significant part.

What had been simmering away under the surface for weeks was something he now had to face. Maybe he did have some kind of learning disability. If he was honest with himself, it had occurred to him a number of times. He'd been on some of the dyslexia websites. But he'd been too ashamed and too scared to take it any further. And when Jamie had so spectacularly and disastrously brought the issue out he'd rebuked in revulsion regressing further into himself.

How could he ever be a journalist if he'd some kind of 'disease'?

Little steps. He would need to dig deep to not only find the courage to go head-to-head with Ryan but also to make amends with Jamie. He could see now what she'd been trying to do. She'd only wanted to help him and he'd rejected her big time.

Luke wiped his eyes and took in a deep, determined breath. Tomorrow he would make everything right.

# Chapter 24

Luke drove over the railway crossing and cruised into town.

The party was still in full swing at Kelvin's although things were looking ominous as a police car pulled up outside.

Luke had been drinking earlier and he didn't want to get caught up in any clashes so turned back onto the main road.

The rain pelted down. He could just make out the lone figure of a woman on the footpath.

It was Jamie, her long black hair glistening.

Whatever he did next would propel Jamie back into his life and he was ready.

He inched the ute along the curbing until he was beside her and opened the window.

She squinted at him and yanked her head away.

"Get in," Luke commanded.

"Go away." Jamie increased her pace.

"You shouldn't be out here alone at this time of night. Get in!"

"I can look after myself."

Jamie stopped walking and Luke stopped the ute.

"Please get in," Luke pleaded.

Jamie hesitated.

Luke swung the door open letting in the cold rain.

She jumped in.

Luke put the ute into gear. Before long they were out on the open road. The ute's tyres swished and the wipers thudded back and forward accentuating the strained silence.

Luke drove around the streets without any purpose. The clock on the dashboard showed 1:00. Luke sighed. This drive to nowhere couldn't last all night.

Luke struggled to say something but he couldn't think of the words or how to start. Maybe Jamie would say something first.

His clenched hands relaxed on the steering wheel. As the minutes passed the chance of another explosion from either of them diminished.

Luke cleared his throat. OK, here goes. "What were you doing out in the rain at this time at night?"

"I needed to think."

Luke risked a glance her way.

Jamie stared out the side window. "Please take me home." It was a bare whisper.

Without a word, Luke pulled over to the side of the road, executed a U-turn and drove back to town.

He parked outside the flat and turned off the engine.

The rain tapped-tapped on the roof.

Luke ached for physical contact. Did Jamie feel it too? Could they bridge the gap? Luke's hand, with the barest of movement, searched for Jamie's. Her hand lay limp then with a small reflex she gave Luke's hand a gentle, reassuring squeeze.

"Come inside," she whispered.

Without speaking any further, they made their way into the flat. Jamie disappeared, remerging as she towelled her hair dry.

Luke paced back and forth. He strode over to Jamie and pushed her back against the wall. She gasped. He brought his hands up to rest on either side of her head, leaning in towards her, his breathing so rapid he was almost hyperventilating.

Luke stared into Jamie's eyes, searching for a sign that continuing would be OK.

She wavered uncertainly for a moment but reflected back in those eyes was the desire she was struggling to resist. She grasped his T-shirt and pulled him closer.

Their lips met in an intense passion, wiping away all the heartache. Jamie moaned, giving Luke all the encouragement he needed. His tongue played with hers, accentuating the force of his hunger.

Time vanished into nothing as the fiery kiss lasted forever. Luke broke away first. He gazed into her eyes, "Don't ever desert me again." He hugged her hard.

Without saying a word, she took him by the hand and led him to the bedroom.

***

Their lovemaking was urgent and passionate.

"Slow down," Jamie said. "It's not a race."

"I can't get enough of you."

"Mmm," she mumbled lazily. "That's because you're experiencing your first make-up sex."

"It's all fine by me."

As his mouth moved further down her stomach and his tongue licked her navel piercing, she guided his head back towards her face.

"Hey, eager boy," she said softly. "That's as far as you go."

"I guess I'm kind of pushing it."

They both laughed.

***

The insistent and loud banging on the front door stirred Luke out of his sleep. One eye half-opened. Jamie wrapped a cardigan around her and slipped into jeans.

Through the open bedroom door, Luke caught snatches of Ryan and Jamie in conversation.

"Is Luke here?" Ryan demanded, the authority evident in his voice.

"Yep, good morning to you," Jamie replied, with sarcasm. "Yeah, he's here."

"Is he all right?"

"He's exhausted."

"Exhausted from doing what?"

"Let him be," she said. "He needs some time out."

"I think I should be doing something but I don't know what," Ryan said, his voice caught.

"Just give him some space. He needs someone to be there for him."

"Can't that be me?"

"Luke's just working through some stuff and that includes you." She paused. She said, more gently, "Can you trust me to look after him for awhile?"

"I'm worried about him." Ryan's voice cracked.

"Give me your cell number and I'll text you later today. I think I might be able to get Luke to open up. But I'm not pushing it," Jamie said.

Luke didn't pick up the rest of the conversation. He presumed Ryan and Jamie were swapping phone numbers.

So Ryan did care.

He winced as he covered his eyes with his hands trying to block out the light.

Hot ball bearings jangled around in his head making it thump unmercifully.

Jamie gave him a Panadol.

He closed his eyes tight, rolled over onto his side and then slept solidly for the next 12 hours.

# Chapter 25

Luke woke again early evening. Fried onions, garlic, tomatoes, bacon and potatoes cooking made his stomach rumble. Man, he was hungry.

He sat up, shaking his head to rid the fuzziness. What had he dreamed? What had been reality?

"Hey sleepyhead." Jamie poked her head around the bedroom door.

"Hey."

"I thought you'd gone to dreamland and weren't coming back."

"What's the time?"

"Almost 7. I've just had dinner but there's heaps left over."

"It smells good."

Jamie wandered over to the bed and sat on the side.

"How are you feeling?"

Luke rubbed his head. "A bit spaced out but OK."

"Ryan was here earlier."

Luke stiffened.

"It's OK," she said. "He knows that you're here and he's OK about that."

The last encounter with Ryan was still larger than life. His older brother had lost it, pain tearing at him, making him the same as Luke. Human with flaws, imperfect, someone who had feelings too.

Jamie looked amazing as always. Her hair was tied back in a ponytail and her T-shirt and shorts displayed long, brown legs, the epitome of summer.

Luke pulled Jamie towards him and she scrambled under the sheets.

They lay in silence for a few beats listening to the Saturday night traffic hum along the main street.

"I'm sorry for everything," Jamie burst out. "I'm sorry for upsetting you in front of your brothers. It was totally insensitive of me. I don't know what I thought I was doing." She rolled over to face him.

Luke's eyes searched her face seeing the genuineness of the apology that laid behind the anguish of her mistake.

"I was wrong." Jamie touched the side of his face. "I wanted to say something to you afterwards to make it up but then Quinn…"

Luke looked away and as the tears welled up for the hundredth time, Jamie held him. He snuggled into her and the tears flowed. Jamie squeezed him tight. She was now crying too. He returned the hug harder, their tears blending together.

"Everyone leaves," Luke finally said when both their tears had subsided. "First it was my folks. Now Quinn. I feel bit by bit I'm being abandoned."

"What you've been through were horrible, horrible things to happen. Anyone who tells you they understand can't possibly, unless it's happened to them."

Luke propped his head up on his hand. Jamie was about to reveal something that he didn't know.

"When I was four, my parents died in a plane crash. I was then raised by the greatest of foster parents. They treated me as if I was their own daughter. I never wanted for anything but always deep down I'd have this sadness that I've never been able to shake, that at any moment it could all be taken away. They would not want me anymore or they would die too."

Luke closed his eyes tight. Jamie had lost her parents too. He reached out to wipe a tear away from Jamie's eye.

"I'm sorry about your folks." Luke held Jamie's hand.

"We have a lot in common, you and I."

"I thought I was going to lose you too."

Jamie frowned. "What do you mean?"

"I thought you'd leave me and hook up with Marcus."

Jamie looked away. "I'm not interested in Marcus but I'll be honest. I was flattered by his attention. But I see Marcus now for who

161

he is. He's out for a good time and he tries it on with any woman. I'm not into that. It's you I care for."

That meant so much to Luke. To know someone understood him and woke up each morning with that person being their first thought.

"Does the pain ever go away?" he asked, toying with the edge of the sheet.

"Not completely. Some days it's not there, ever. Other days it's all I feel. But because my parents died in a plane crash I'm completely freaking out about flying to South Africa. I've never been on a plane before." Jamie paled.

This was a surprise. The super-confident Jamie scared of something?

"But don't worry about me," she said hurriedly. She ran her hand over Luke's forehead. "Let me ask you something. What helps you? What is it that makes your pain a little bit bearable?"

One word was the answer to everything. Barely audible, the word escaped from Luke's lips. "Write."

"Then go write."

A rush of air escaped from Luke's mouth. Why had he been waiting to do the thing he loved the most? The one solid thing that would always be there. The one thing no one could take away from him. The one thing that would never abandon him.

***

After Luke ate the leftovers, Jamie suggested a walk along the beach.

They held hands and strolled along the foreshore seeking warmth from each other as the air whispered an autumn chill. There were few people about, the cosiness of inside a more attractive option.

When they got back to the flat there was a black sports bag outside.

"Ryan must have dropped it off," Luke said as he rummaged inside. There was a change of clothes, toiletries, his MP3 player and he'd even chucked in some chips, crackers, some fruit and his journal.

"That was nice," Jamie commented.

Luke picked up the bag and they went inside.

Jamie sat down at the computer and Luke pulled up a chair beside her.

"I did want to talk to you about this dyslexia thing. I think I've been in denial," Luke said.

"All I wanted to do was help you but my approach was all wrong." She threw her hands up in frustration.

They spent the rest of the evening trawling through websites on dyslexia.

Jamie read out a whole heap of symptoms and while he didn't have all of them it did explain a lot of things that had always been a mystery to him.

"Look at this!" Jamie said. "Here's a list of careers for a person with dyslexia. Vet, lawyer, engineer, dancer, singer, psychologist, astronaut." They both laughed at the idea of Luke as an astronaut.

"And I can't dance to save myself," Luke added.

"Well then, look," Jamie said, pointing at the screen. "You'll just have to be a writer or a journalist."

Jamie must be kidding around with him but there on the screen in big letters the words 'writer' and 'journalist' blared out at him.

"You can be anything you want."

A whole world was opening up to him.

Jamie flicked to another website. "Here's a list of famous people who are dyslexic. Jamie Oliver, Orlando Bloom, Tommy Hilfiger, Richard Branson. And look at the authors – Agatha Christie, F. Scott Fitzgerald, Hans Christian Anderson. Hey, maybe there's a reason as to why you like *The Matrix* so much?"

"Why's that?"

"Keanu Reeves is dyslexic."

"Well, there you go." So you could achieve great things. It hadn't stopped Keanu and it wouldn't stop Luke either.

"We need to work out what to do now." Jamie typed some words into Google. "Diagnosis of dyslexia... dyslexia assessment providers... parents to talk to teacher... classroom assessments... observation surveys... It's amazing you've got this far through the education system and nobody has picked it up."

"Yes, maybe school has failed me and I could get angry about that but what's important now is to get help so I can no longer be held back."

Jamie looked at Luke. "You realise we'll need to talk to Ryan about this. I'm sure he'll have some ideas on how to handle it."

Luke frowned. "I know. I'll need his support and we need to involve him as he's my legal guardian." He stifled a yawn that set Jamie off yawning too.

"Time to turn in," Jamie said.

Luke fell asleep instantly which was rare for him. After midnight he awoke with a peacefulness he'd been searching for since Quinn had died. Calm waves washed over him and the desire to write burned like an eternal flame. Careful not to disturb Jamie, he tiptoed out to the lounge with his battered, old journal. By the backlight of his cell phone the words flowed on to the page like a light stream of water.

Before he knew it, staring back at him from his journal was a poem.

*Without You*

*I am*

*Nothing.*

*With You*

*The world has a*

*Soul.*

*Without You*

*I am*

*Lost.*

*With You*

*One can*

*Exist.*

*Without You*

*There is no*

*Life blood*

*And*

*Nothing.*

*With You*

*The world*

*Makes sense.*

When he read it back a couple of times he was unsure as to whether the poem was about Jamie or Quinn. Maybe it was about both of them. But what was really clear was that writing was his antidote.

He read the poem over and over, and then something clicked. The poem wasn't about someone. The 'you' was writing.

Luke smiled. He'd written the 'L' in 'Lost' and 'Life' back-to-front. But he wasn't embarrassed. This would be just another challenge in his life he would work hard to overcome.

He returned back to bed holding dear to his heart that his ability to be all that he wanted would never be lost if he just believed in himself.

# Chapter 26

Although Luke wanted to stay at Jamie's forever it was best for him to return home on Sunday night.

He kissed Jamie goodbye and promised her he wouldn't let Ryan get to him.

The next part of the plan was to get an appointment with his teacher and Ryan would need to be involved.

Ryan was in the lounge watching TV when Luke arrived home.

Instead of going out of his way to avoid Ryan like he would have done a couple of months ago, or even a couple of days ago, he made the first attempt at conversation.

"Hey brother."

"Hey brother."

Ryan held Luke's gaze for a moment. No words were required to acknowledge what had passed between them on Friday night.

"Enjoy your sleepover?" Ryan teased, muting the TV.

Luke threw a cushion at him.

"Welcome back. So what's up?"

Luke took a deep breath. Now was the time to put it out there.

"Jamie and I talked a lot…"

"Are you sure that was all you did?"

A warmth spread over Luke's face. He silently thanked the semi-darkness.

Ryan's attempt to use humour to lighten things was a good sign but he ignored the comment.

"We researched this dyslexia thing. We need to make a time to see my teacher."

Luke outlined what their research had revealed. Ryan didn't interrupt. He nodded at various times. For once, Ryan was listening to him, really listening. The walls between them were disintegrating.

"OK. I'll make a call to the school on Monday."

"I want Jamie to come too."

"I'm not sure-"

"Jamie is coming," Luke said, raising his voice a notch.

Ryan wavered for a moment. Was Ryan about to tell him that it wasn't appropriate? "OK. That maybe a good idea."

"Thanks bro."

"Hey, I'm taking Saturday off. Thought I'd borrow a boat and go fishing. Want to join me?"

Ryan taking Saturday off? Luke squinted at him. Was there a hidden motive? Could he handle being with Ryan in such a confined area? There would be no quick escape. Was it only eighteen months ago when all of them would spend the whole day fishing? Enjoying it for different reasons. For Ryan it was probably to escape from the pressures of work. Luke loved the beauty of the Sounds. The wide expanse of the sea surrounded by the hills of deep-green native bush. The abundant animal life, the shags and the seals and if you were lucky, a pod of dolphins darting in and out of the water.

But that was before things had got a lot more complicated and life had dealt some cruel blows.

Luke was willing to give it a shot. "OK."

"Good on you," said Ryan, throwing the cushion back.

When Luke switched on the light in his bedroom, the memory of the torment and its resulting disarray reverberated around him.

Someone had been in here to tidy up. Probably Ryan. Quinn's bed had been made, the mess cleaned up and a lot of the sciencey stuff was gone. The room looked like what Luke needed – clean, tidy, uncluttered. It would take time for him to get used to having the room all to himself. But he fought his initial reaction to want to make Quinn's side look like Quinn would walk right back in at any minute. He was OK with it now.

He put his phone down by the bedside table and there staring back at him was the photo of Luke and Quinn in a brand new photo frame. He picked it up, remembering that day. Quinn would always be in his heart, be a part of him but he still hadn't satisfied a desire to do something sacramental, to find some kind of closure. And he'd keep looking until he found it.

***

The boat cruised into the shelter of Cable Bay, their favourite fishing spot. Ryan killed the motor and Luke dropped the anchor.

They baited their lines, threw them over the side of the boat and waited for the push and pull tugging of biting fish.

A keen breeze whipped up taking away much of the warmth of the sun. The sea slapped gently against the boat and in the distance the ferry's engines thudded as it made its way up the Sounds.

A poem seeped into Luke's head.

*Deep blue ocean*

*Not depths of despair*

*But mystery layers of chance*

*Swirling this way and that.*

*Magic and beauty-*

Ryan's reel buckled. "Woo hoo," he yelled. He furiously wound the reel. Ryan had landed a good sized cod. "I beat you." Ryan stood back admiring his fish.

"Not so fast," Luke responded, as he battled a bucking line. "Why does everything have to be a competition with you?"

"Someone has to be first," Ryan joked.

Luke wanted to argue with that but he let it go.

By lunch-time they had caught four fish each. They good-naturedly riled the other when one of them edged ahead.

Luke gutted and filleted the fish and then popped them into the chilly bin. The day was turning out all right. Not one word slid out that could potentially set the other off.

Ryan had cut lunches and they sat munching on egg sandwiches watching the increase in boats as the day drifted on.

"I was sorting through some stuff of Dad's the other day," Ryan commented.

"Oh yeah."

"There was something there I thought you might be interested in." Ryan pulled some papers out of a plastic bag and handed them to Luke.

He recognised his dad's writing. They were just scrawls really, random notes he'd taken about boats comparing various models and prices.

"I'm not sure why you're showing these to me." Luke turned over the pages, puzzled.

"Take a closer look at the writing," Ryan encouraged.

He studied the childlike scrawl that was not much different to his own. Then it stood out at him. Some of the letters were written backwards.

"It looks like dad was dyslexic too," Ryan said, breaking the silence.

"Gosh," was all Luke could say.

"Did you know dyslexia can be hereditary?"

"No."

"I sometimes wonder if mum and dad, especially dad, were still alive that they would have picked up on your dyslexia sooner," Ryan said, sighing. "I've let you down. I've been so busy concentrating on work to pay the bills over the years that I regret I haven't been there for you or the others."

Two seagulls dipped near the bow of the boat, squawking at each other.

Did Ryan believe he'd failed his brothers in some way?

"No. No. No." Luke shook his head as Ryan off loaded his guilt. "Maybe we haven't appreciated enough of all you've sacrificed to keep us together. It can't be easy." He'd never wanted to dwell on the horrendous strain Ryan must be under, the amount of responsibility he'd shouldered over the years. Of course, Ryan would never say or admit it but why hadn't Luke not picked up on the real reason Ryan snarled and had little patience? The mask he wore fooled everyone.

"Lately I've felt like all of us have been slowly losing touch with each other," Ryan continued, staring out in the distance.

"Me too." So it wasn't just him that imagined the links that held them together were rusting away. "Maybe Marcus and I need to make more of an effort to ensure you're not working your butt off every day."

Ryan laughed. "Hey, I took this on with my eyes wide open. And don't you think I've regretted any of it. I've only ever wanted you guys to make a reasonable fist at your education so you can get a good start in your working life."

"I know."

"I'd want mum and dad to be looking down on us happy you were doing good, that I'd done good for you." Ryan flicked some fish scales off the rail.

"They would be. I know they would be but Ryan I can't meet your ideal of what you want me to be. You want to push me down a road that I don't want to go down, that I know is not right for me. I don't have that academic brilliance everyone else in the family seems to have got that I somehow missed out on. I don't want to fail you but I need to do stuff on my terms."

"You and I are different but you persist in fighting me every step of the way."

"I don't think we are that different. Family is important to you. If it wasn't for your determination who knows where we'd have all ended up. You work your guts out every day to prove that. Family is important to me too. I'm not stupid enough to say I wish things could go back to the way they were before but I miss that closeness we used to have. Like we'd stick by each other to the end. I don't like the way we've all been living like we're going through the motions, being one step removed like satellites suspended in perpetual darkness."

Ryan chuckled. "You're not going to start spewing poetry at me, are you?"

In the past, Luke would've wanted to bite back at Ryan but now he ignored it. It was his right to express himself in a way that was OK for him and if Ryan didn't get it then he would keep working on it until one day Ryan would understand too.

"I haven't seen Cherie much lately."

"Yeah, well. I don't think she'll be around much anymore. I need to call her to remind her to pick up her stuff."

"Hey, sorry it didn't work out."

Ryan gazed out over the sea. "It's just one of those things. I don't really have the time for a serious relationship. I think she was feeling neglected."

A boat rocketed past; the passengers waved. Luke waved back. *I think we've all being feeling neglected. Including Ryan.*

"I noticed the reframed photo of Quinn and me. Did you do that?" Luke asked.

"Yep."

"Thanks. We need to make more time to talk, you and I. I mean really talk and not just sparring off one another."

Ryan nodded. "Don't think I don't get you. I do. You're sensitive, vulnerable. I want to protect you from any more hurt. You've been hurt enough."

The two seagulls rested on the stern, silent, having settled their differences.

Luke coughed. So Ryan did get him even if it was just a little.

They didn't need to say anymore. That one small gesture of Ryan taking the time to show Luke his dad's handwriting had sown the seeds for a better relationship with his brother.

*** 

It kind of went without saying that it was expected that Luke would be back at school on Monday. He wasn't looking forward to it. The clammy hands and trembling lips brought back his fear. Tight shoulders emphasised his tension. He'd got behind in all his work but the upcoming appointment with his teacher on Wednesday would sort out the awful, tangled mess he'd gotten himself into.

He skipped algebra; he was so far behind now it would be impossible to catch up. The only bright spot was that he'd a new book for English and was eager to share this with Jamie.

After school he ran down to The Book Vine.

"I haven't read this book," Jamie said, skimming the blurb.

"When can we start?"

"How about you get going on it tonight and we'll pick it up after school on Thursday?" Jamie ran a duster over the sci-fi section. She coughed. "Don't ask me the last time these shelves were dusted. How did the fishing trip go?"

"Good. We came nowhere close to killing each other."

"Things are looking up then?"

"We're talking and that's got to be good." Luke smiled.

"I think I need to throw these out," Jamie said, as she picked up the vase that held the once pretty flowers Luke had picked for her. She tipped the brown and crispy foliage into the bin.

"Pickings are slim in my garden at the moment, my fair lady," Luke teased.

"Well, maybe we could make some flowers. Someone dropped off a book this morning about how to make paper flowers. Then I'd have permanent flowers."

Luke liked that idea. Something permanent in his life at the moment would be good.

Luke light-footed it home. He passed the back door and the recycling bins, and stopped short. He spied the journalism brochure he'd asked Ryan to look at a number of weeks ago poking out from behind a pile of newspapers.

He bent down to pick it up wiping the top of it on his shorts where some OJ had spilt on it. His spine prickled. Was this what Ryan had thought of the brochure? Had he even read it? How could he so carelessly discard it just because it wasn't Ryan's choice? Did this mean they were back to the start again?

"Hey brother."

Luke whirled around.

It was Braydon.

"Hey little brother. How's it going?'

"Cool. They've got more kittens down at the animal shelter. Do you think Ryan will say 'yes' to one?"

"Gee, I don't know." Luke pushed open the back door. "What do you think Trixie will think about a new cat?"

"She'll be fine," Braydon replied with certainty. "Do you want to come down to the shelter with me tonight? I can show you the kittens."

"Sorry. I've got some stuff to do. Maybe later in the week."

Luke could've kicked himself when Braydon's smile disappeared from his face. Was he turning into Ryan? No time for his brothers, dismissive.

"But maybe later," Luke quickly added. "How did you get on with that book assignment you had to do?

"It was OK. I think I could've done better though. But I've another one due in a couple of weeks."

"How about I give you hand with that?"

"Really? You've got the time?" Braydon's eyes widened in surprise.

"Sure. I should've helped you the first time around."

Something else had been tugging at him lately and maybe it was time to make the change.

"Do you want to sleep over in my room this weekend? It gets lonely without Quinn," Luke said.

Braydon's eyes sparkled. "That would be awesome. We could watch *The Maxtrix*."

"How about watching something you'd like?"

"OK. Maybe *Batman Begins* or *King Kong*. Or the movie with the two gay guys. Something to do with a mountain."

Luke smothered a grin. "Maybe we'll check it out with Ryan first."

That night the usual dinner banter returned although there was a sense of incompleteness with the now permanent empty place at the table.

After dinner Marcus and Braydon scuttled outside to kick a ball around and Luke got up to start loading the dishwasher.

"Not so fast. I want to talk to you," Ryan said.

Luke stopped in mid-step. The hairs on the back of his neck stood up at the frostiness in Ryan's voice. What had he done now?

Luke sat back down. He wracked his brains for any clue that might indicate what this was about.

He risked a glance at Ryan eyeing the hard look and concrete set of his jaw.

This didn't look good.

"Is there something you'd like to tell me?" Ryan asked.

"I... I... I'm not ..." Luke stuttered.

"Let me refresh your memory. I had a phone call today from a...," Ryan paused while he referred to a notepad where he'd written down a name. "A Susan Meyer from the National Association of Journalism checking some details on a scholarship form that I had apparently signed as your guardian."

Luke's blood ran cold. Shit! He'd completely forgotten about that. That had happened a lifetime ago. Would Ryan, once again, put a roadblock in his path?

"Is there anything you want to say?"

"I'm sorry. I shouldn't have done it. I was just angry at the time." Luke paused. "It wasn't very smart, was it?" He expected the usual rant and rave, a dressing down, a grounding or maybe he'd be shipped off somewhere.

Ryan remained silent.

Luke kept his eyes fixed on the table and fidgeted waiting for Ryan's outburst.

"Would you do it now?" Ryan asked.

"Do what?" Luke asked, confused.

"Forge my signature? Go against me?"

"No. It was a stupid thing to do. I was determined to get my way."

"I can see that. I can be just as strong-minded as you."

Silence filled the air again.

"I've given my permission for the scholarship application to proceed to the next step."

That completely blew Luke away.

"Thanks," Luke managed to say at last, lifting his head to look his brother in the eye.

Ryan leaned closer to Luke. "Let me make it very clear to you," Ryan said, the words dripping ice. "Ever pull a stunt like that again and I'll kick your arse so hard you won't be able to sit down."

Luke nodded. His breath escaped slowly. It left him in no doubt that no one crossed Ryan Conway and that included his own brother.

Luke rose from the table again. "Oh, I have something for you." He retrieved the brochure he'd left hidden under a pile of papers on the kitchen bench.

He set it down in front of Ryan. "I think you misplaced this."

Ryan stared at the brochure. He looked up at Luke.

Their eyes met and locked.

No further words were needed.

***

Luke hung back after English class and waited for his classmates to leave.

"Luke," said Mr Bligh. "What can I do for you?"

"There's something I need to show you." Luke pulled his old journal and some notebooks out of his backpack. "You remember you asked me about whether the work I've been doing is original?"

"Sure. And you told me it was. I believe you."

"I guess I needed to settle any doubt in my mind as well as yours. I wanted to show what I've done to prove I haven't cheated."

"You don't have to do this."

"I do." Luke stood steadfast. He opened up his journals and placed them firmly on the desk. "See here. This was the inspiration for the flash fiction competition." He pointed to the page. "As was this one here…" He opened up his other journal and flicked to the correct page. "…which I combined with this one…" Luke flicked back a few pages. "…and here are my original notes for the essay."

"Luke, stop. It's OK." Mr Bligh placed a hand on Luke's arm. He picked up the journals and studied the pages. "This is good work. You obviously like to write poetry."

"I do. I know the writing looks weird but it seems I've got dyslexia. I'm seeing Mrs Stevens soon so I can get some help," Luke rattled off without a breath.

"Thank you for sharing your writing with me. I hope the next steps go well for you. Let me know if I can help."

"Thanks, Mr Bligh. I just wanted to clear up the whole thing about the cheating."

Luke popped the journals into his backpack and walked out of the classroom with his back straight and his head held high.

***

Luke's head spun after the appointment with Mrs Stevens. The light at the end of tunnel burnt stronger. Things had gone well.

Mrs Stevens put things in motion for Luke to have a dyslexic assessment undertaken.

In the meantime she acknowledged that it was no point in Luke continuing with algebra because of his low grades. Luke could've hugged her.

Talk turned to Luke's career options.

Mrs Stevens had picked up on the change in body language, the fire in his eyes when he talked about writing and his desire to become a journalist.

Discussions turned to the application for the journalism scholarship, the writing of the flash fiction competition. The good marks obtained in the book report proved that Luke certainly had a talent.

A significant shift in thinking came from Ryan. While Luke had expected resistance from Ryan in the re-channelling of his school subjects, he accepted that it was best to work with Luke's strengths.

Afterwards Ryan took Luke and Jamie to Café Salt, where they drank their coffees and reflected on the meeting.

"It was unfair of me to have kept pushing my ambitions for you," Ryan admitted, stirring his coffee.

Luke and Jamie glanced sideways at each other. This was a real concession on Ryan's behalf and not an easy admission.

"You'll have to put in a lot of work to catch up on your new subjects," Ryan warned.

"Yeah. I know but I get extra time now to complete my assignments and Mrs Steven said I can listen to audio books which will save a lot of time. And this extra class before school with other students who have dyslexia will be great." Luke brimmed with so much enthusiasm he couldn't stop talking. "And all those other good techniques Mrs Stevens suggested like highlighting important stuff, using flashcards to help my memory and I really need to start writing lists."

Luke caught the grin that passed between Ryan and Jamie.

"What?" he said.

"It's good to see you back to your old self," Jamie said.

"Yeah," Ryan agreed. "I have to admit. I don't know much about creative writing but I can see potential."

Luke beamed. Words of encouragement and praise from his brother. It had been a long time coming but worth every moment of waiting.

# Chapter 27

Luke made a side trip into the tattoo studio on Thursday.

The tattoo guy remembered him from a week ago. "You've come back for the forms, right?"

"Yeah. This is something I really need to do."

"Understand. It gets like that. Once you have an idea of getting some ink it's hard to shake," the tattoo guy said, handing Luke the permission forms and samples of the Tree of Life tattoo.

That night while Luke summoned up enough courage to approach the subject with Ryan, Ryan gave him the perfect opportunity.

"I know we haven't mentioned much about your birthday on Saturday. I thought we could have a low-key thing here. Invite a few mates around. I heard the other guy who was in the car with Quinn is out of hospital now."

Luke didn't know what to do about his upcoming birthday. He kind of wanted to celebrate turning 17, but without Quinn…

Ryan waited for a response and when none was forthcoming blurted out, "Forget it. It's too soon. I shouldn't have mentioned it."

"No, no, that's fine. Something without too big a deal would be OK. Actually there is something I would like to do for my birthday."

"Yeah, what's that?"

"I want to get a tattoo."

The words were hardly out of Luke's mouth before Ryan shot back with, "Absolutely not."

"Why?"

"You're too young."

"No, not good enough. Marcus got one when he was seventeen."

"Maybe in a year's time."

"You haven't even asked me what kind of tattoo I want."

"It doesn't matter; you're not getting one."

"Can you at least hear me out?"

"OK, what's the deal?"

Luke showed him the Tree of Life tattoo and explained how this would be his tribute to Quinn.

"I know you want what's best for me, I get that. But I need to be able to start making some of my own decisions. And this time I'm doing it right, responsibly."

The straight set of Ryan's mouth discouraged Luke. Ryan stared out the window, lost in thought. "I'm sorry I didn't listen to you first. It's a fine thing that you want to honour Quinn in such a way..."

Was Ryan going to say no? "I need your permission before I can get the tattoo," Luke said, thrusting the sign-off forms and a pen at Ryan.

Ryan took the forms and placed them on the table. He ran his finger down the permission form, tapping it when he came to the place where he would need to sign.

The waiting was killing Luke. Please sign, please sign, please sign. The words kept time with Ryan's tapping.

"You're right," Ryan said, scrawling his signature. "And I can see you've given this a lot of thought."

Luke had expected more of a fight on his hands and had been prepared to dig his toes in but Ryan was making an effort.

"How about this be my birthday gift to you?" Ryan said, handing the forms back to Luke.

Luke's mouth dropped open. This was a complete turnaround. "Well, the money thing…"

"Don't you worry about the money. I can work something out."

"That would make it a very special birthday present."

Ryan ruffled Luke's hair. "When you were thinking of getting this tattoo?"

"Tomorrow."

"Tomorrow!"

"I'd like it done to mark the end of being 16 and turning 17."

"I'll come with you."

"I don't need anyone to hold my hand."

Ryan stifled a laugh. "You've never been that great with pain."

"True," Luke acknowledged.

"I'd like to be a part of this," Ryan said, his laughter subsiding.

Luke caught the serious tone in Ryan's voice.

"I promise I won't say a thing."

"That's hard to believe," Luke mocked Ryan.

"I promise I won't say anything much," Ryan corrected and they both laughed.

Things moved quickly. The next morning Luke rang the tattoo studio and Tyler, the tattoo guy, booked him in for that afternoon.

Luke texted Jamie.

*Luke: Getting a tatt this arvo. Wish me luck!*

*Jamie: OMG! Can't w8 2 c it.*

*Luke: I'm worried about the pain* ☹

*Jamie: You'll be rite. Suck it up, big boy!*

And it hurt like hell. Luke bit his lip. Ryan snickered and said, "I told you so."

"Swear as much as you like," said Tyler, "I've heard it all before."

Luke was lying face down on the table. The first ten minutes weren't so bad, more like Trixie digging her claws lightly into him.

He grimaced as the needle dragged once again across his shoulder, stinging and burning the skin.

The pain dulled. Luke figured that it was probably the adrenaline kicking in.

"You still alive there brother?" Ryan asked. "I haven't heard you groan for at least five minutes."

"Yep. It's just all numb now. I think I'm paralysed."

Ryan and Tyler laughed.

"No pain, no gain," said Ryan.

Two hours later it was all done.

"Do you want a photo?" Tyler asked, as he applied a hot towel over the tattoo.

"Yep," said Luke gingerly, getting up. Stars flitted inside his head from lying on his stomach for so long, from holding his breath, from the pain.

"Here's a mirror," Tyler said, handing it to Luke.

Luke studied the medium-sized tattoo that spread out over the top of his back, the branches pointing towards his shoulders. Tyler had done a great job. It was exactly what he wanted – the compact tree brimming with leaves and with life. A tiny root system poked out from the bottom. Under the tree, was one simple word, 'Quinn'. Luke blinked away a tear.

Ryan patted him on his shoulder. "A great move buddy."

Tyler took a photo of the tattoo and one of both Luke and Ryan.

"Some things about looking after your tattoo," Tyler said, rubbing in some ointment. "Keep the bandage on for at least two hours. Moisturise it regularly. It might get itchy – try not to scratch it. Some slight scabbing – don't pick. Showers, no hot baths. And the rest is in this leaflet here."

"Sure," said Luke, carefully putting his T-shirt back on.

"Well, that wasn't too bad then was it?" said Ryan, getting into the ute.

"Apart from the pain, it was a breeze," Luke replied sarcastically, then changed to a more serious note. "Thanks for coming. Maybe we could get the photo of the two of us framed."

"Yeah, I could-" Ryan's cell phone rang. "Ryan here. Yes… That's great…" Ryan glanced at Luke and smiled. "OK…. Sure…. I'll tell him… Thanks for ringing."

Ryan put the phone down. "You're not going to believe this."

"What?

"You know the journalism scholarship you… I…. We… applied for."

Luke nodded. Butterflies crisscrossed in his stomach in unison with his crossed fingers.

"Well, it seems you've just been awarded a year's scholarship towards the National Diploma in Journalism."

"Are you sure?" Luke's words slipped out in a croaky tremor.

"Yep. That was Susan from the Journalism Association. More details to come but she noticed on the app form that it was your birthday tomorrow. She thought it would be a good birthday present."

What could he say? Was his writing really that good enough, that other people could see he'd what it took to be a good writer, to become a journalist? He let out a big sigh. His world spun. Wild visions and images of him writing for the world's top newspapers went running through his mind. He could work towards becoming a journalist, documenting storm chasers just like Michael Sharp. The possibilities were endless...

"A journalist in the family."

Luke could only just make out the words but he caught the modest delight in Ryan's voice.

When they arrived home Marcus had already picked up the pizza and there was the familiar commotion of dishing out the food, the pouring of drinks and the opening and closing of cupboard doors and drawers.

Luke showed Marcus and Braydon the photo.

"Great tatt," said Marcus, nodding in approval.

"I bet it hurt," chipped in Braydon.

"We have some great news to top today off," Ryan said. "Everyone grab a drink."

Marcus threw Ryan and Luke a beer each. Braydon poured himself a lemonade.

"Actually I've never liked beer," Luke said, throwing the can back to Marcus. "Is there any wine?" Luke asked, turning to Ryan.

"Must have," Ryan replied, as he wandered over to the smaller fridge kept in the laundry that held the drink supplies. He rummaged around inside.

"How could I work in a vineyard and there not be any wine?" Ryan grumbled. "Ah, here we are. A 2004 Resolution Bay chardonnay."

Ryan poured Luke a glass and proposed a toast. "To Luke – a tattoo and a journalism scholarship and not yet quite seventeen. We're proud of you Luke."

Luke grinned. The compliments kept right on coming from Ryan.

The brothers tipped their cans and glasses together.

Marcus and Braydon wanted to know more about the journalism scholarship so Luke filled them in.

"Sounds cool but can we eat now? The pizza will be getting cold," Braydon said.

"Yep."

"Let's get to it."

"Who's got the bread?"

"Why are there mushrooms on this one…"

"I'm sure the pizzas are getting smaller or am I just famished…"

*** 

Luke hadn't slept well Friday night. His shoulder ached. Mentally he couldn't quiet his rambling mind and physically he was drained from yesterday's excitement.

Snoring noises coming from Marcus's bedroom next door before midnight indicated a rare early night for his older brother.

As dawn broke he snuck out of the house.

The last of the autumn flowers meandered in the garden. He picked a few of them admiring the patterns of light forming prisms on the drops of dew.

He strolled on down the drive and in ten minutes he was at the cemetery.

He was pleased there was nobody else around. He wanted to share this time alone with Quinn.

The white cross with Quinn's name on it rose out of the freshly turned over dirt. He placed the flowers in one of the jars.

He knelt down on the dirt. "Happy birthday Quinn," Luke whispered. "Miss you heaps."

A tear escaped from his eye and fell onto his hand. "I got a tattoo for you."

The flute-like song of a bellbird broke the stillness of the morning.

"Well, you were right about the writing. I won a scholarship." The words sounded foreign as if someone else was speaking them.

"I also wrote a poem about me, you and me," Luke's words caught in his mouth. "It's kind of about writing too. It fits lots of scenarios. I should stop blubbering and just read it."

Luke took a deep breath, wiped his hands over his teary eyes and recited his poem.

When he'd finished, he sat there for a while longer. More birds had joined in the bellbird's chorus. The changing patterns of light danced in the trees.

He stood up, brushing the dirt off his jeans. He needed to get back home soon. He didn't want anyone, especially Ryan, to worry.

He lifted his head towards the sun coming up over the hills and he knew for the first time in a long time that things would work out OK. He smiled. His first day as a seventeen-year-old held all the promise he needed.

# Chapter 28

Loud banging from the garage distracted Luke. He headed over towards the garage and popped his head around the door.

"Kind of early to be working on a Saturday," said Luke.

Marcus appeared out from under the car.

"Luke," Marcus said. He reached out to grab a rag and wiped the grease off his hands. He struggled to his feet.

"Happy birthday bro."

The two brothers grabbed each other's hand and shoulder bumped.

"Ouch!" exclaimed Luke.

"Still a bit tender, huh?"

"Not the best of nights. You were home early for a Friday night."

Marcus didn't reply. What was troubling him?

"No girls?" Luke asked.

"Nah. Giving that a rest for awhile."

Another silence hung between them.

"You know, I wasn't after Jamie," Marcus said.

Luke said, "You could've fooled me."

"I admit. It began that way. I enjoy the chase. You know that. But after Quinn died all I was trying to do was fill some gap. Something was missing. I don't know…" The words trailed away.

Marcus fiddled with a wrench.

Luke had understood Ryan the least but Marcus was turning out to be an enigma too.

"It didn't work though," Marcus continued. "It just left me… empty."

"We were all trying to find something to ease our pain," Luke said. "I don't know after all we've been through why we didn't reach out to one another. We haven't let things come between us before and it shouldn't now."

"We just need to look out for each other more," Marcus said.

"Anyway, what was the story with that blonde at the party?"

"Helena? Yeah, she's in your face. It's like she's constantly on the prowl."

"Well, rather you than me. I thought she was going to eat me alive."

"She might go for all the poetry and ramblings you write."

"Ramblings?" Luke raised an eyebrow.

"You know, that mumbo-jumbo you churn out. Chicks dig that sort of thing."

"Mumbo jumbo?" Luke chuckled.

Marcus turned a slight shade of red. He was making a light-hearted attempt to appreciate Luke's own talent.

"Where are you at with the car?" Luke nodded, peering into the engine bay.

"I could teach you a thing or two about car maintenance."

Luke screwed up his nose. He'd no interest in cars. They were just a means to get from A to B. He was about to turn away but changed his mind. If they were to heal he needed to do his bit too.

"Sure, although don't get too cocky asking me to pass wrenches and screwdrivers and stuff."

"I'm sure you're not that bad. Maybe you could spit out one of your poems and I'll give my interpretation on the meaning."

"Yeah, yeah, yeah. You'd probably put some weird twist on it."

They both laughed.

Marcus threw an arm around Luke's shoulder.

"Poetry and mechanics. There's the title for your next poem. See what you can do with that," Marcus said, throwing Luke a wrench.

Luke held the words in his head as they whirled and twirled, taking on a life of their own. The mechanics of poetry. Poetry and mechanics. He liked it. But he pushed it away so he could fully concentrate on the lesson that was about to begin on carburettors.

# Chapter 29

In keeping with Luke's wishes, Saturday was a low-key celebration/remembrance day.

Jamie had texted Luke earlier wishing him a happy birthday and inviting him to dinner at the flat that night.

He was busting to tell her about the scholarship.

When Luke arrived at Jamie's she was just opening a bottle of chardonnay.

"Mmm. Smells good," he said, as he walked into the kitchen.

"There are breads and dips for an entrée, steak and veggies and a special surprise for dessert."

"Wow! You've been busy," Luke said, pleased at the effort she'd gone to. He kissed her. "You look nice."

"You look pretty good too."

"Marcus's birthday present to me. He said now that I am officially dating I needed to spruce up."

"Oh, did he?" Jamie laughed, admiring the new dark denim jeans, light blue shirt and sweater.

Jamie poured the wine and they started on the bread and dips.

"How are you feeling - about today?" she asked tentatively.

"OK." He sighed. "I'm kind of glad it's almost over. I was dreading it to a point but we had a good afternoon. We had a few people over. It was a bit awkward to start with but once the food came out things loosened up." Luke didn't tell Jamie about his visit to the cemetery. He wanted to keep that to himself. "I was definitely looking forward to tonight."

"I should think so. Slaving over a hot stove all day," Jamie teased.

"I have some good news." Luke stopped for dramatic effect.

"Well... I'm dying in suspense here!"

"You are now looking at a journalism scholarship holder."

"No!" Jamie squealed, covering her mouth in delight. She threw her arms around Luke. "I knew you could do it. Luke, I'm so happy for you."

"I don't know all the details yet but it looks like I'll be off to tech next year."

"I'm so proud of you." Jamie hugged him tighter.

"It'll be hard with the dyslexia but I guess that's some stuff I can work on now to prepare me for next year. At least I'll be doing what I want to do and not what Ryan wants."

"What did he say?"

"He wasn't quite so demonstrative as you but I think he was secretly chuffed."

"Hey, I'm glad things are going better for you two. When do I get to see this tattoo?" Jamie said, changing the subject.

"Given that I'd have to take my shirt off and who knows where that may lead to…"

Jamie punched him playfully on the arm.

"…you'll have to settle for a photo for now."

Jamie studied the photo.

"Did it hurt?" she asked.

"A wee bit," he bluffed.

Jamie served up dinner and they dug in.

"That was yummy," Luke said, complimenting Jamie on her cooking as she poured herself another glass of wine.

"Hey, what about me?" Luke asked, gesturing towards his empty glass.

"You're driving remember?"

"I thought I'd be staying the night," Luke hinted.

"Did you just?" Jamie's eyes danced. "Does Ryan know you had invited yourself to stay the night?"

"I dunno… I didn't really say… I just assumed…"

"Well, if you're dead keen on staying the night you'd better let him know otherwise you'll wind him up."

"True."

Luke texted Ryan.

*Luke: At Jamie's 4 the nite.*

*Ryan: Stay safe.*

"I have a surprise for you," Jamie said, her eyes glowing with excitement, "but it'll require me to blindfold you."

"OK," Luke replied, raising his eyebrows. "Is this some kind of weird sex game?"

"You wish." She laughed. "Trust me. Now turn around."

Jamie tied a long red scarf around Luke's head, covering his eyes.

"Can you see anything?"

"No. It's completely dark."

"Good. Now, take my hand."

Jamie guided Luke's hand into her warm one and led him towards the back of the flat.

Luke took tentative steps to avoid tripping over anything.

"Stop," she said.

Raspy metal on metal indicated a curtain was being pulled back. More metal as a key turned in a glass door.

Somehow, through the disorientation of not being able to see, Luke guessed they were at the part of the flat where it joined with the bookshop.

"OK." Jamie took Luke's hand again and pushed open the door.

He breathed in the familiar and comforting mustiness of old books.

"Keep coming," Jamie said. "Now there's a table here and a seat here. Can you sit in the chair?"

"Mmm," Luke replied.

"I'll be back in a minute. No peeping!"

Luke sat in the dark. What crazy thing was Jamie up to now? Plates clashed together and cutlery tinkled. The glass door closed. A match scraped against a box, acridity releasing.

"Are you ready?"

"Yep."

"Ta da!" Jamie exclaimed as she untied the blindfold.

A huge cake covered in chocolate icing sat on the table in front of him, bathed in candlelight. 'Happy Birthday' shone up at him.

"Oh my God, Jamie."

His mouth fell open.

Seventeen candles burned brightly.

"Make a wish. Hurry!"

Luke took a big breath and blew out the candles all in one go.

Jamie clapped her hands. "Don't tell me what you wished for but I presume it had something to do with writing?"

Luke just nodded. It was true. His goal of becoming a writer or a journalist was more in reach now than a couple of months ago.

Luke cast his eyes around the inside of The Book Vine.

Jamie had lit candles everywhere and their faint glow threw eerie shadows across the room. She'd tied some balloons around some of the book stand ends and there was a shiny banner with 'Happy Birthday' on it, hanging across the front counter.

"You know how we talked about what heaven would be like – books, a fireplace, hot chocolate, a cat?" Jamie said softly. "Well, this is the next best thing for today."

"I love it," Luke replied.

The flickering candle light emphasised Jamie's face.

"The shop feels completely different. It's like we're in our own secret world." He couldn't think of a more wonderful setting for his birthday.

Luke cut the cake and they devoured a big slice, licking their fingers as the chocolate icing melted.

"I think I'm drowning in chocolate," Luke said. "This is overkill."

"I hope you enjoyed your birthday," Jamie said, getting up.

"It was pretty good."

Jamie took Luke by the hand and led him over to the couch. She looked like a bronzed beach babe in the golden glow of dancing light.

She took off her top.

"You want to do it here?" he asked incredulously.

Jamie nodded her eyes sparkling with mischief. "Remember this is the next best thing to heaven."

"And I won't argue with that!" said Luke. He loved every bit of her craziness.

His sweater and shirt hit the floor landing next to her top.

# Chapter 30

Everything went into overdrive over the next few weeks. Luke had an assessment done for dyslexia. The results would take a couple of weeks to process. In the meantime Luke attended his first additional pre-school class.

As he entered the classroom, students had settled down to work. Some of them had their backs to him. The blonde hair of the girl he'd known since kindergarten swayed as she talked.

"Caitlin?" Luke asked.

Caitlin turned around. "Luke!"

"What are you doing here?"

"Well, it seems I have dyslexia. I'm taking extra classes to help increase my 'learning potential'," she said, putting two fingers in the air to emphasise the quotation marks. "What gives with you?"

"Same."

"Hey, I knew we were special people. Want to sit next to me?"

Caitlin pulled up a chair and then introduced him to the others at their table. Luke nodded in their direction.

News had got around school that Luke had won a journalism scholarship. Students walked past him in the school corridors and patted him on the back congratulating him. Luke nodded at them. He had some sort of relevance on earth. He was not just the guy who couldn't do algebra, the guy whose brother was killed in a car crash or the guy 'doing' the new chick in town. He'd also received an invitation to join the student newsletter team. The editor thought it would be a great idea for him to write about his scholarship and provide regular updates from tech next year.

***

And it so happened that all English classes at Haven River High were taking part in poetry week. At the end of Luke's English class Mr Bligh asked him to read out one of his poems.

"I don't know. I'd rather not," Luke protested.

"Come on," came the encouraging cries of his classmates.

A red haze crept into his vision. His breath quickened. Flashes of the *whack, whack, whack* of a ruler, and cruel taunts from Andrew and Zack invaded his mind.

Luke turned his head to the side. He would've loved Jamie to be here but it was Caitlin's slight features that smiled back at him.

Luke sighed. "OK." He could do this and now was the time to put away the ghosts of his past.

"Yay!" The class clapped.

Luke walked to the front of the room, took a deep breath and met a steady gaze of smiling faces.

"This poem is called Indigo Sky and is inspired by the unique weather that precedes a storm in Haven River."

Luke cleared his throat. He recited his newest poem. Was that his strong confident voice ringing out?

The faces that stared back expressed different emotions. There was a respectful silence as he neared the end.

"-Indigo Sky

The last goodbye

For you and I."

Luke finished. He wiped a hand over his forehead where he'd been sweating. He waited for a response from Mr Bligh and his classmates.

"Woo hoo!" someone yelled out and started clapping.

"Yeah, right on!" yelled someone else. The room erupted in a frenzy of clapping and stamping.

Luke's face broke out in an ear-to-ear grin.

He'd done it. The loud clapping pushed the *whack, whack, whack* down, down, down and out of his life forever. He'd conquered his fear and now there was only a light burning brightly in front of him.

\*\*\*

Luke dropped around to Jamie's flat after school on Thursday catching her in the middle of sorting things into boxes.

"What are you doing?" he asked.

"I'm packing."

"Where are you going?" Luke searched Jamie's face for an understanding of what she was doing. "You're leaving?"

"I was only staying for three months, remember?" Jamie said, placing a hand on Luke's arm.

"But... you can't... I thought...," Luke stammered, the old uncertain Luke returning. He hung his head. "When do you go?"

"I'm on the Sunday afternoon's ferry." Jamie avoided Luke's eyes as her own teared up.

"So soon. Why didn't you say something?"

"I know. I should've. I've been wanting to but there never seemed to be the right time. You've been happier over the last few weeks. I didn't want to spoil that."

"Can you stay longer?" he pleaded. "I feel like a hole has been ripped out of my heart. How can I keep going without you? You're my rock."

"I fly out to London on Monday and then onto Jo'burg. I bought the ticket months ago. I can't stay." Jamie touched his shoulder. "I didn't know I'd get involved with anyone, with you. I'm sorry."

"Everyone leaves," Luke whispered. He stared blankly ahead with the sense that, yet again, someone important was leaving his life.

"Luke, there are lots of ways for us to stay in contact. South Africa isn't that far away. You've got so much to look forward to. Life is taking shape for you now. Before you know it you'll be winging your way over to the other side of the world reporting on the latest celebrity scandal," she said, forcing a light-heartedness into her voice.

"I know. I'm just being silly." Luke sniffled.

"Come here," she said softly.

He moved into her open arms.

They stayed locked together both lost in their own thoughts.

"I wish you could stay forever," Luke whispered into Jamie's ear. His heart cried - his first love, being wrenched away from him so soon.

*** 

Luke and Jamie spent every moment they could over the next week together and pretended their time wouldn't be ending shortly.

On the Saturday, the day before Jamie's departure, Luke had planned to work on some school projects in the afternoon and spend Saturday night with Jamie.

Although autumn was in full swing, summer had decided she wasn't letting go easily. The last three days had been hot but there was a strange heat today.

Luke looked outside his bedroom window. Minky grazed; nothing much changed there.

The sun hid behind the clouds which hung listlessly in the sky. The trees stood in shy silence. It would swing to the nor'west at some stage. The beginnings of the familiar arch of dark cloud were forming parallel to the blue sky. The hot, dry, dead heat air combined with the last few nights' full moon had a restless and breathless quality. The air closed in on Luke, suffocating him.

There was only one place where he would be able to breathe easier.

He sprinted down the stairs, grabbed the ute keys and cruised on down the road.

*** 

The wind cavorted through the open windows instantly reviving him.

Luke stared up at the sky willing for a change, something to break the impasse. He was in the mood for the weather to let loose, to cleanse everything around him. Like when he'd have to clean his room, a good storm settled him.

He slowed down and turned off the highway. After he drove over the railway crossing he came to a stop in the clearing.

He alighted out of the ute breathing in the coolness of the forest. The water that was Haven River gushed but this time there wasn't anything blocking its way. No fallen trees or snagged branches. Its path ran freely with purpose. Moving, changing, but persistently keeping on its straight and narrow journey despite what obstacles fell in its way. Here was the surety of life. That whatever happened, Haven River would keep flowing, and ebbing too.

He wandered over to the swimming hole and dipped one hand in the opalescent water. He moved his hand. The ripples started out as one and then multiplied, spreading across the surface. Shaking the water droplets off, he strolled back to the clearing. The last time he was here was with Jamie.

Luke raised his head. Tyres scrunched on the road and they were getting louder.

He shielded his eyes against the sun and frowned. He wanted to be alone and wouldn't welcome the impending intrusion.

But as the vehicle grew larger, he smiled. This was no intrusion. This was Jamie.

Jamie parked the jeep next to the ute.

"What a surprise," Luke said, as Jamie climbed out of the jeep. "I would never have expected to see you here."

"It was so hot and I was lost and restless. I needed some time by myself…" She struggled to finish her sentence.

"Same," Luke said, putting his arm around her, drawing her close. "This place has a lot of happy memories for me. You'll always be part of that now. I'll never forget you. You were my first love, first time."

Jamie wiped away her tears with the back of her hand.

"I'm sorry," she whimpered. "I'm being silly."

"No, you're not being silly," Luke said, squeezing her tighter.

They stood in silence for a moment.

"We're still on for tonight, right?"

"Of course."

"Do you want me to see you off tomorrow too?" Luke asked.

"I don't know. I'm not great with public good-byes. I'll just end up a blubbering mess."

Luke was kind of glad she wasn't keen on the idea. He'd cry too.

"I'm still anxious about getting on that big plane," Jamie said.

"I know. It'll be fine. You really are worrying over nothing."

"Oh! I have something for you," she said pulling away from his embrace. Jamie made her way over to the jeep leaving Luke anticipating what it was she'd for him.

She removed a package from the front seat. "I was going to give this to you tonight but I think this is where it's best to say goodbye."

She handed him the brown paper bag. "This is for you."

Luke reached out for the bag and peered inside. He straight away recognised the item.

"Oh, Jamie," he said. Was this for real? It was the leather-bound journal in the shop that he'd admired so much a number of weeks ago.

Luke pulled the journal out of the bag. It looked even better now than it did in the shop. He caressed it with his hand and inhaled the combination of the new leather and paper.

Jamie laughed. "See, we're mad. What makes us want to smell paper?"

Luke burst out laughing. "We're not mad."

He opened the journal up to the front page.

"I've written inside it for you. 'To Luke. Write until you can write no more, Love Jamie'."

"Thank you," he said, hugging the journal to his chest. "I'll treasure it forever."

A blackbird on the willow tree eyed them from above.

"I really don't want you to go," Luke said, grabbing Jamie's hand.

"I know." She leaned forward touching her forehead against his.

"I don't know how I'll be able to do this without you."

"You will and when all seems lost remember your creativity, your words, your writing. No-one can ever take that away from you. Have faith and trust in that ability. It will always see you through."

"I'll miss you like crazy."

"So then how did you want to spend our last night together?" Jamie asked, pulling away from Luke.

"Remind me again what The Book Vine looked like in candlelight?"

"Mmm. I'm sure I could dig out the candles again."

"Great idea. You know what. I don't have a photo of you. Let's get one of us together. We can take a selfie."

Luke pulled out his phone and with their arms around each other he snapped a couple of photos ensuring that the long, continuous path of Haven River was in the background.

***

*One week later, Saturday night*

The familiar chaotic scene played out in front of Luke at the family dinner table and he smiled.

Plates of food were passed around with Marcus and Braydon scrambling to pile the largest potatoes on their plate.

Ryan tapped into his cell phone, Marcus's cell phone went 'ding' and Braydon's eyes wandered over to the 6 pm news on the TV.

Luke itched to speak up about the loss of connectedness and sense of family that had been bothering him for some time. He wouldn't have said anything before, before life had changed big time. But with his new growing self-confidence he wasn't sitting back anymore. Now was the time to say his piece.

"For heaven's sake," Luke said, above the noise. "Can we at least eat one meal without people checking their cell phones and watching TV."

Bowls poised in mid-air. Ryan and Marcus stopped in mid-text and Braydon's head swung back around.

"What's that?" Marcus asked.

"Guys, remember the times dinner was only about us. A time for us to, you know, catch up, talk."

"Yeah, I do," said Ryan, placing his cell phone down on the table.

"I kind of miss it," Luke added.

"So do I," Braydon said, flicking his eyes over his brothers.

"It's what kept us together. We should never forget that."

"Well said, Luke," said Marcus. "You're now the official keep-us-in-line-at-dinner person."

"You don't need to go that far but since you've suggested it, turn your god-damned phone off," Luke said, swiping Marcus across the arm.

"Luke has a point," Ryan said. "Let's put some effort into this. From now on no more cell phones at the table and the TV remains off."

Braydon got up and switched off the TV.

216

"And you," Ryan said, pointing his fork at Luke, "no swearing at the table."

"Yes, sir." Luke mock-saluted Ryan.

Luke had made another stand and because of that the bonds of brotherhood strengthened again.

After dinner everyone somehow ended up in Luke's bedroom. Well, it was kind of Luke's and Braydon's bedroom now. Braydon had moved in, occupying the side of the room that had once been Quinn's. It had been strange at first but Braydon and Quinn had similar personalities. Hanging out with his younger brother was cool. Braydon kept his side of the room tidier than Quinn that was for sure. Luke chuckled to himself.

They were also joined by the newest member of the family, Gertie. Ryan had given in and a seven-week old tortoiseshell kitten was now Braydon's constant companion.

"Let's watch a DVD," said Braydon, flicking through Luke's DVD collection. "Can we watch *Brokeback Mountain*?"

Without waiting for a reply he'd pulled the DVD out of the case and placed it into the player.

"Eww!" Marcus protested. "Isn't that about-"

"Yes!" they all chorused back.

"It doesn't matter that it's two guys," Braydon said. "They loved each other. And as Luke's love is on the other side of the world it might cheer him up."

"Not likely. But good try. I think I might just do some writing. You can watch it though."

"I'd better stay. It does have a M rating," said Ryan, studying the front cover.

"I don't need supervision. Remember we've all had to grow up faster than a lot of other kids." Braydon settled himself down on his bed.

"Well, regardless I'll just hover in the background in case there are any questions."

Braydon rolled his eyes and chucked a cushion in Ryan's direction.

Ryan jumped onto Luke's bed. "Push over."

Luke skedaddled over to make more room.

Marcus gave in and fell on his stomach on Braydon's bed. "I'll catch up on some shut-eye."

"What? The girls will be missing you," Ryan said.

"I've chosen to spend Saturday night with my bros. You should be thanking me for my company."

They all groaned, and Luke chuckled. This was the closest his family had been since Quinn had gone.

Ryan picked up a book sitting on the table.

"Did you finish this?" Ryan asked, turning *The Summer Now Ending* over in his hands.

"Yeah. Remember I had to write a book report on it? It was funny, and a little coincidental, that the theme of the book was about following your own path and not bowing into what other people want for you."

"OK. If there was a hidden message in there I received it loud and clear," Ryan said. "You know, I am proud of you. Mum and dad would've been proud of you too."

"Thanks. That means a lot."

Ryan put the book back down. He punched the pillow and readjusted his head. Already soft snoring sounds came from Marcus's direction.

Luke glanced at the photos sitting on top of his desk. There was the reframed photo of two cheeky grins of him and Quinn on their thirteenth birthday, the photo of him and Ryan at the tattoo studio, one of his folks, and the newest addition, him and Jamie at Haven River.

He'd finished his old journal a couple of days ago. When Jamie left, the inspiration had left too.

He reached over to the leather journal sitting beside his bed. He stared at the cover and slowly turned to the first page. He read Jamie's inscription – again. How many times had he read it over the last week? He picked up his pen and the words rushed out:

*My family is healing once again. And I'm healing too. I know now where life is taking me. It's the only direction, the right direction.*

*The write direction.*

# Acknowledgements

Many thanks to the following people. I couldn't have done it without you.

Lesley Marshall, who provided valuable critiquing on plot, content and heaps of other stuff!

Lindsay Carlton, my beta reader – thanks so much for your time, effort and suggestions.

Lynn O'Shea, for designing the awesome cover.

Kristen Kieffer at shesnovel.com. Your blogs and articles were so helpful in keeping me on track. Thanks also for your encouraging emails.

# About me

Casey Fae Hewson lives in sunny Marlborough, New Zealand. She loves to write young adult and contemporary romance fiction. When she's not reading, she'll be mountain biking, walking, gardening and listening to music.

Connect with me

http://caseyfaehewson.com

Friend me on Facebook: http://facebook.com/caseyfaehewson

Follow me on Twitter: http://twitter.com/@caseyfae

Follow me on Pinterest: https://nz.pinterest.com/caseyfaehewson/

Instagram: https://www.instagram.com/caseyfae8917/

Love to read? Love to write? Be the first to read about my latest book release and my reading and writing life. Sign up for my newsletter for romance readers, The Romantic Heart when you visit.

# Coming soonish!

## Aqua Bay

## How far would you go to protect the place you love?

Nerissa Taylor, a dolphin eco-tour guide, will leave her beloved Aqua Bay at the end of summer to live in the city and marry her fiancé, Scott.

Geologist Jackson Darnell arrives in Aqua Bay to investigate oil exploration possibilities hiding behind a cavalier attitude to avoid the pain of his past.

When Nerissa and Jackson's paths cross, sparks fly as their goals clash.

Increasing tension forces Nerissa to question what she wants in life and face a frightening unresolved issue. And she is determined to prevent Jackson from getting anywhere near the sea and the precious dolphins.

Can Nerissa convince Jackson that what he's doing is wrong before it's too late?